D0757928

RING IN THE NEW

RING IN THE NEW

by

E.

PHYLLIS BENTLEY

Ring out the old, ring in the new
TENNYSON: IN MEMORIAM

LONDON
VICTOR GOLLANCZ LTD
1969

Printed in Great Britain by
The Camelot Press Ltd., London and Southampton

AUTHOR'S NOTE

Ring in the New continues the story begun in *Inheritance* and continued in *The Rise of Henry Morcar* and *A Man of His Time*. The Oldroyds, Bamforths, Morcars and Mellors are shown striving to put their ideals into action, in the changing conditions of the modern world.

Halifax
August 1968 to January 1969

THE OLDROYDS

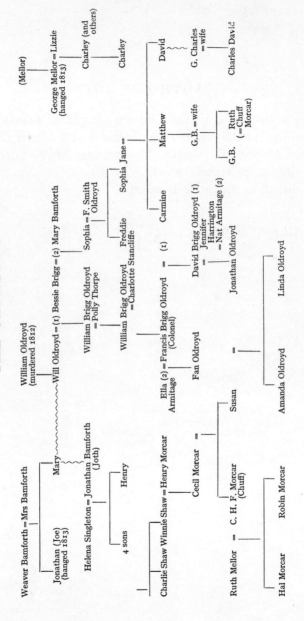

CONTENTS

I

THE OLD ORDER CHANGES

1

A GOOD WAY TO GO

It was always a bit of a nuisance to catch this early morning London train, thought Morcar, drawing his car neatly between the white lines of the last empty parking place at the station, and applying the brake. One had to wake at the right decidedly early hour, bath, shave, dress, open the garage, drive the car the necessary miles and—most difficult of all—find a parking space. If one arrived too early the cars of the men returning to Annotsfield overnight by sleeper were still in position; a few minutes later they had gone, but the men going to London by this, the first good train of the day, were pouring in to fill the spaces. Indeed Chuff, Morcar's grandson, grumbled about his attempting this train at all; later ones, he urged, would serve just as well. But this train had many advantages. It was very fast; to reach London from the textile West Riding in under three hours was really splendid. One could keep a business appointment—perhaps two—in the morning, do a business lunch and a couple more business appointments in the afternoon, catch the evening express and sleep in one's own bed that night and be at the mill first thing next morning. That the train gave a good breakfast and had all seats bookable was also, of course, advantageous, but Morcar made nothing of that; it was business he was after.

These modern young sprigs had no idea what getting business meant in the way of work, he reflected between derision and indulgence as he turned to lock the car; if his grandson Chuff thought a man starting from nothing achieved Syke Mill and Old Syke Mill and Daisy Mill by catching trains at ten o'clock in the morning, he could think again. But catching this train was a bit of a bind, to tell the truth. Still, he had caught it, thought Morcar, smiling happily; he had arrived at exactly the right moment. He put his car keys in his pocket, drew out the necessary silver and turned towards the car park attendant with his customary lively springing step.

His shoe caught on one of the rough protuberances of the stone paving—put down in Victorian times and never since repaired. His ankle twisted and he was thrown violently sideways, his heavy brief case dragged him down, then flew out of his hand; he crashed full-length to the ground.

"Ee, Mr Morcar!" cried the attendant, running towards him. "Ee, I am sorry! Are you all right? Are you hurt? You! Come and help him up," he shouted, waving to the transport policeman who stood near by.

Morcar was not a particularly heavy man, carrying no superfluous fat, but the two men had some difficulty in raising him, for he seemed unable to help himself. He hung in their arms, flaccid. A grey fluid crawled, viscous, from above his ear to the collar of his handsome London-going suit. His eyelids blinked, his mouth gaped a little, but he did not speak.

"Shock," opined the policeman. "I'll fetch a chair."

"You'd best 'phone them at Stanney Royd," said the car attendant uneasily.

Between them they managed to prop Morcar on the chair inside the car park attendant's little hut, and the policeman telephoned for an ambulance which soon arrived.

By the time Chuff arrived at the hospital, however, driving with the speed of panic down the Ire Valley, Morcar was dead. The strong impact of the millstone grit against his temple had fractured his skull.

2

GRIEF

"OH, NO. OH, NO!" exclaimed Jonathan when Chuff telephoned him the terrible news. The month being August, he was at home for the holidays before taking up his new teaching post in the south.

His tone was heartbroken, and Chuff found himself feeling irritated.

"He was my grandfather, not Jonathan's," he thought. "These Oldroyds!"

Of course, he was an Oldroyd himself, on his mother's side, and proud of it, but the rest of him was Morcar; he had none of that suspect Bamforth streak, which, surviving down a century and a half even though now mingled with Oldroyd blood, made his half-cousin Jonathan, in Chuff's opinion, soft in the wrong places.

"Shall I tell Susie?" said Jonathan quietly.

Chuff groaned. The thought of the grief which his unstable little sister would feel at the loss of her very dearly loved grandfather filled his whole body with anguish. All the same, he felt Jonathan would break it better to Susie than he would himself; they could weep in each other's arms, he thought savagely, and say soft things such as he could never utter.

"Yes, tell her."

"Should I ask Mother to come down, do you think?"

What would be the good of that? wondered Chuff irritably; everyone at Stanney Royd knew that Susie detested Jonathan's widowed mother, who had recently remarried; the two were mutually jealous of Jonathan's affections. Or if we didn't know it before, we know it now,

thought Chuff; somehow Morcar's death had drained the
daylight from the sky and substituted a livid distorting
clarity. "Why ask me about your mother, anyway?" he
continued silently. It then occurred to him that probably he
was his grandfather's heir and Stanney Royd might well be
his. Trust Jonathan to know the proper courtesies in these
matters. "Do as you like," he said roughly. "I think I'll
telephone Ruth." At the thought of his betrothed, for the
first time he felt moisture behind his eyes; in this hour of
misery he needed her so greatly.

"I could fetch her, but I don't think I ought to leave
Susie," said Jonathan.

"No, stay there, I'll fetch her myself when I can get away
from this place."

He supposed the best way to tackle these frightful things
he had to go through was to behave as one did when entering
the dentist's, and say: "In an hour or two this will be over."
But, just as at the dentist's, it didn't really help; the ordeal
still remained to be endured. First there was Ruth and her
mother. Mrs Mellor opened the door of their flat to him; the
early hour, and Chuff's face, warned her of disaster, and she
looked at him in question.

"My grandfather's had an accident. He's dead," blurted
Chuff.

"I'm sorry. He was a good man," said Mrs Mellor
composedly.

Ruth coming up at this point threw herself on Chuff's
shoulders and burst into tears.

The two things together, Ruth's sympathy and Mrs
Mellor's calm dismissal of Morcar to the ranks of the dead,
maddened Chuff.

"Come along, Ruth," he said roughly, removing her arms
from his neck, though at the same time savouring to the full
their loving warmth. "You must come to Susie."

Ruth, who knew the need well enough, ran to get her handbag, while Mrs Mellor said gravely: "Yes, indeed."

"I think I'll ring up Syke," said Chuff. "It'll be a while before I can get there. Nathan's usually there about this time."

Mrs Mellor led him to the telephone and left him.

"Nathan," began Chuff.

"Oh, Mr Chuff! Oh, Mr Chuff!" cried the works manager, frankly weeping. "I've heard! We've all heard! It's all over Annotsfield. Oh, how could he! How could it be, Mr Chuff! Surely it can't be true?"

Somehow this was soothing.

"I'm afraid it is true, Nathan," said Chuff, and though he winced as he spoke, he gave a detailed description of the accident such as he knew the old man would appreciate.

"Shall I put the flag up at half-mast, Mr Chuff?" asked Nathan solemnly when this account was closed.

"Aye, do that," said Chuff, using a Yorkshire word consciously for the first time in his life—it seemed appropriate to the occasion.

As he drove Ruth along the Ire Valley, the Syke Mill flag was visible in its mournful position—Nathan had lost no time.

Then there was Stanney Royd, with everyone soaked in grief. Jonathan's mother, Aunt Jennifer, now Mrs Armitage, sat by the fire with bowed head, tears rolling heavily down her cheeks. Her husband, Nat, stood beside her quiet and still, very much the gentleman; he had heard the news at his mill and rushed home to bring his wife down to Stanney Royd. He stepped forward and offered Chuff his hand.

"I had a deep respect and affection for Mr Morcar," he said. "If there's anything I can do to be of help, Chuff, you'll let me know?"

"Thanks," said Chuff.

His aunt turned aside her head in a weary motion of

distaste. It struck Chuff that Morcar's death had returned her to the period of her first love, her first marriage, her first husband's death in the War, when Morcar brought her and her child from bombed London to the safety of Stanney Royd; her second husband seemed to her at the moment an irrelevance. Ironic, thought Chuff, grinning sardonically as he bounded upstairs to Susan's bedroom. Ruth stood in the open doorway, looking anxiously for Chuff, not venturing to go in. As he expected, his sister lay face downward, motionless, on her bed, her thick mane of pale golden hair tossed about her shoulders. Jonathan sat beside her, grave and sad, holding her hand. Or rather, his hand was clutched feverishly in hers; there was tension in every line of her fingers.

"Susie," said Chuff softly.

Susie rolled over and sat up. Her beautiful face, usually of exquisite line and delicate colouring, was now puffed and blurred; her dark blue eyes were red with weeping. She turned a blank look on her brother, then fell back into her previous position as if exhausted. Chuff gave Jonathan an enquiring look which said "Hysterics when she heard about grandfather?", and Jonathan gave a slight affirmative nod. Susie did not move again, and Chuff saw that she did not want either himself or Ruth; she did not want anybody but Jonathan. He repressed a twinge of jealousy firmly, telling himself he must always do, he always wanted to do, the best he could for poor little Susie, and left the room, pushing Ruth rather strongly ahead of him.

"Don't you want to stay with Susie?" murmured Ruth in his ear.

"No. She's got Jonathan. I must go and see the solicitors— he may have left instructions about his funeral."

"You must have some breakfast first," said Ruth quickly, and she went off to direct the distraught Mrs Jessopp to prepare it.

The wretched day dragged its slow length along. Chuff,

who had conducted the obsequies of his grandmother under Morcar's supervision, knew what had to be done and did it competently. The solicitor, the registrar, the undertaker, the vicar. Jonathan demurred over the religious service—"Uncle Harry was not a believer in the Christian faith," he said—but Chuff overbore him.

"We have to do things decently and in order," he said, and he arranged for a service in Marthwaite Church with six men from Syke Mills to act as pall-bearers and all the usual accompaniments of choir, organ, flowers and so on. After the service, the crematorium, in accordance with the wish Morcar had expressed in his will. The drive there would be a longish one, and Chuff proposed that the women of the party should omit this and return from the church direct to Stanney Royd. He said this for Susie's sake, but Susie indignantly repudiated the suggestion.

Chuff found the most trying feature of that day, and the one which followed, to be the endless enquiries and condolences which came to him by telephone. He had to tell the story of the accident over and over again: to the family, to the men at the mill—Nathan sobbed—to the Mayor of Annotsfield, to every man in textiles (it seemed to Chuff) in Annotsfield, Bradford, Halifax, even Leeds and presently some in London. At first this was in a way rather a relief; the narration seemed to lift the burden a little, accustoming him to a tragedy for which he had not been prepared. But as the day wore on he began to feel that the words—so banal, so terrible—would choke him if he had to utter them once again. The way they were received also sometimes exasperated his inflamed nerves. Jonathan, for instance, said gravely:

"Well, it was a good way for him to go."

"Nonsense! That's nonsense, Jonathan!" raged Chuff. "How can you say that? Such a waste!"

"He was engaged in what he cared for most: textile business," said Jonathan as before.

Chuff muttered in fury, but the next time someone on the telephone said sadly: "Ee, it does seem a waste; it does that," he flew out angrily and told them that Morcar had died at his post, so to speak; he would have liked nothing better, Chuff was sure.

Many people, of course, uttered appreciations of Morcar which consoled Chuff. "He was a grand man—straight as a die—I knew him when he was at Annotsfield Tech—always a good designer, you know—ideas of his own—yes, I remember when he began his Thistledowns—he was a fine chap—one of the best—quite a romance, really, how he rose up from nothing, you might say."

Chuff, repeating this last tribute to the family circle with shy pleasure—"he feels that if Morcar could do that on his own, he can do the same," thought Jonathan with his usual perception—was infuriated when Jonathan said:

"As Hardy said: 'Every man's life seems a poem when you look down into his grave.'"

"There was nothing poetical about grandfather!" shouted Chuff angrily. "He was a practical man all through."

"You don't understand what I mean," said Jonathan.

"Oh, yes, I do."

"Have it your own way," said Jonathan wearily.

"I will," said Chuff, glaring at him.

Eventually, by putting Ruth on the telephone at Syke Mill, Jonathan at Stanney Royd and Jennifer at Emsley Hall, the enquirers were suitably dealt with while Chuff was absent making necessary arrangements.

In the evening there was a long obituary notice—really a very fine one, so that Chuff felt proud—in the *Annotsfield Recorder*, and friends from other West Riding towns rang up to say there were agreeable references in their local evening papers. Next morning a short but well informed piece actually appeared in the *Yorkshire Post*.

"I ought to keep these, I expect," said Chuff uneasily to Ruth.

"I'll cut them out for you," said Ruth.

Thank goodness Ruth was there; what he would have done without her Chuff could not imagine.

3

FUNERAL

AT LAST THE night—which Jonathan spent wakefully, thinking with remorse of sharp utterances he had perhaps made to Morcar, while Chuff slept the sleep of exhaustion—was over; the morning hours crawled by, and the funeral began. It was a tremendous affair; the Iredale Road was black with cars, the police had great difficulty in marshalling them anywhere near Marthwaite Church and many textile notabilities had to walk several hundred yards in a drizzling rain.

The English are good at ceremonies, reflected Jonathan; they are decorous, they have a great sense of what is fitting and proper; they are patient and do not push, they do exactly what they have promised to do, they don't get excited, or weep obviously, or sing hymns loudly; they pay attention to what is going on and show respect by a grave demeanour. The beauty of the words of the Prayer Book funeral service is really outstanding. The hymns today were well-chosen, the flowers handsome, the vicar's address short but adequate; Chuff, who with Susie of course led the family cortège into the church, looked no longer a lad but a responsible young man, blunt featured, determined, well able to cope with anything which might require action. Susie looked so exceedingly beautiful and so fragile that every male heart in the church, Jonathan felt sure, yearned over her. Ruth and her brother G.B. looked grave but stolid, in complete self-control. Jennifer wore mourning, perfectly plain but of the highest elegance; Nat, limping beside her, looked what he was, a soldier and a gentleman of high integrity, but not really a textile manufacturer. Nathan and Mrs Jessopp wept quietly. In a word—"and I have noticed this before," thought Jonathan—"people behave on great occasions like themselves."

As he stood there, very still, his eyes suitably cast down, he allowed his thoughts to roam over the history of his family, which had now again come to a turning-point. In 1812 the Luddites of this valley, protesting against the introduction of cropping frames into their hand industry, led by George Mellor, in spite of the protests of Joe Bamforth, a man innocent and mild, had murdered a millowner, William Oldroyd. Though the murderers were hanged and the Oldroyds prospered, through the vicissitudes of loves and hates kinsmen of all who had played a part in that evil deed stood in this church today. He himself, of mingled Bamforth and Oldroyd stock, held firm to what he regarded as Bamforth principles—peace, brotherhood, tolerance. Ruth and her brother were Mellors; though not in the least a murderer, G.B. had an aggressive note which increased as he grew older. Into the Oldroyd-Bamforth-Mellor story had come Henry Morcar, a man of great textile skill, determined, able, clear-sighted, not blinded by hate, but alienated from his wife and son—by her doing, Jonathan felt sure, though he did not know that story exactly. He reflected with a little bitterness that Chuff and Susie Morcar were children of this alienated son. Morcar had loved, too late, Jonathan's grandmother, whose photograph in the prime of her great beauty always stood alone in his private room. When she perished with her husband in a London air-raid, Morcar had rescued her daughter Jennifer, then with child by her Oldroyd husband, and brought her to live in safety in the Ire Valley with himself and his old mother. Her child was Jonathan, and he remembered well now in this sad hour how as a toddler he had trotted along the Stanney Royd paths, his hand in Morcar's, chattering and pointing, relying in complete unthinking confidence on Morcar's love and care. It came on him like a flash:

"He loved me better than he loved Chuff."

He remembered his curt refusal to enter Morcar's beloved Syke Mill, and mourned.

"One should be kind to people while they're alive," he reflected. "Afterwards it's too late."

The service concluded, and the coffin was carried from the church.

4

WILL

AFTER THEY HAD committed Henry Morcar's body to the flames—the crematorium was a cold, empty, varnished sort of building and the service was to match, thought Jonathan; he was reluctant to prefer the Anglican ceremony, but in fact did so—the family party strove to eat an admirable luncheon at Stanney Royd and then gathered in Morcar's den to hear his will.

Susie had suddenly become very talkative over lunch; her face was flushed, she related anecdotes, and at times even laughed at them. Jonathan well understood the rising hysteria which this indicated, but Chuff, he saw, was displeased, and Mrs Mellor and his mother in their different ways also showed dissatisfaction. When the party quitted the table Susie suddenly left them and ran away upstairs. Jonathan contrived to slip after her, unobserved, and caught her at her bedroom door.

"You must come down, Susie."

"I don't want to."

"You must, Chuff will be hurt if you don't."

Susie sighed, but went down meekly.

Jonathan perceived that Nat Armitage and Mrs Mellor had disappeared.

"Shall Mother and I withdraw, Chuff?" he said.

"Don't be silly," said Chuff irritably.

They grouped themselves about the lawyer, Jennifer and Jonathan in silent accord taking a more remote seat than the rest.

Morcar's testamentary dispositions were, except for a few

small items, simplicity itself, and, thought the lawyer, thoroughly fair and what was to be expected. The very considerable residuary estate was divided into three parts. Chuff inherited one third, Susie another third; the remaining third was divided between Jennifer and Jonathan. Considering the various relationships involved, and the events of Morcar's life, it seemed a good arrangement. But after he had announced the bequests of a handful of Syke Mill shares to the works manager, Nathan, and a pension to Mrs Jessopp—which were both well received—he noticed, as he had so often noticed on these occasions, that the principal beneficiaries did not look too pleased. Only Mrs Armitage appeared quite contented. Jennifer was indeed grateful to Morcar, not only for his allocation to her of the income from a specified sum, which she had more or less expected, but for his benevolence in giving her the independence of the sum outright. But Susie looked blank and cross; being under age, she would be subject, until her majority or marriage, to her brother's administration for some years; she knew nothing about money, but wished to be responsible only to Jonathan.

On the other hand, Jonathan wore a look of cold distaste. "I don't want any Morcar money," he said irritably to himself. "I'm not related to him. I don't believe in the capitalist system of inheritance. I can make my own way. But I suppose I'd better keep my share, in case Chuff loses all the rest, trying to manage Syke Mill—which is all too probable. I needn't spend the money," he thought, brightening. "I can save it up, keep it for Susie when she needs it."

Chuff fixed his eyes on the electric clock on the mantelpiece in an attempt to keep cool, but in fact he was crimson and frowning. The largest number of Syke Ordinary shares were his; Jonathan and Mrs Armitage had none, but only investments, impeccable though perhaps less lucrative, outside textiles; Jennifer had a few Preference, Susie of course a large proportion of both Ordinary and Preference. Chuff understood that his grandfather's wealth lay very largely in his mills and machinery, and that this source therefore had to be tapped to provide for Susie. He regretted this but accepted the necessity; he would try to buy them out one of these days, though no doubt he would have to sell Stanney Royd to do it. But it was not this which maddened him. No! It was Jonathan's situation.

"If he marries Susie, and of course he will, he'll get control of her third as well as his own sixth. He'll have more of grandfather's stuff than I shall."

He tried to quell this mean thought, but could not, for he was furious.

"There's one good thing, even if only one, about all this," said Chuff mournfully as he drove Ruth home that night. "That new ring road is off, for the time being anyway. I shan't have to see Syke Mill pulled down and find somewhere else to go."

This was true. At first the threat of the new by-pass to the fabric of Syke Mill was said to be imminent; in two years at most the clearance of its route would have begun. Then there was a hitch about the plans with the Ministry of Transport, and the word *postponement* was wafted vaguely through the Annotsfield air. Then there came a national financial crisis; *priorities* were now the cue, many large schemes were abandoned in face of others considered more essential. Now, *it will be eight years at least*, said people in the know; and presently, after another national financial crisis, *eight* became *ten*. Morcar gladly, and Chuff sadly, then gave up all thought of new premises for the present.

"If I'd had that to face as well, I don't know how I should have managed; I don't really," continued Chuff in the same mournful tone.

"But Chuff, I don't think you ought to feel a martyr about

your Syke responsibilities," said Ruth, bracing as ever. "It's a trust, a challenge."

"That's what *you* think," said Chuff crossly. It was on the tip of his tongue to confide to her his vexation about Jonathan's sixth plus third, but he was ashamed to do so, and refrained. "Ruth wouldn't understand," he said to himself, and he felt vexed.

5

HOUSE AND HOME

"I SHALL BE off to Ormbury next week, of course," said Jonathan. "But would you mind if I stayed over the weekend, Chuff? Mother seems a good deal upset, you know. I think I ought to be near her. But I don't want to go and stay with her at Emsley Hall, really. Would you mind?"

"What are you talking about?" said Chuff irritably. (But even as he spoke, he knew.) "Stanney Royd's your home, isn't it?"

"Not now, I think."

"I shall be glad if you'll continue——," began Chuff.

"No. It's awfully good of you and I appreciate it tremendously. But it wouldn't work, Chuff. You'll be getting married, you know. A man wants his house to himself."

"Well," said Chuff in a tone of acceptance, feeling a sudden unexpected rush of pleasure. "But what about Susie?" he growled, turning his head aside.

"I shall always come to Annotsfield in the holidays—I'll find some rooms," said Jonathan, adding quickly: "You know my hopes concerning Susie."

"Well," said Chuff. "You're always welcome here, of course."

Somehow the last two words made Jonathan decide that he would never enter Stanney Royd again without a specific invitation. He nerved himself to request that Morcar's photograph of his grandmother might become his own. Chuff coloured, and looking aside, agreed.

6

A NEW CAREER

"WHAT EXACTLY DID Grandfather *do* at the mill, I wonder?" thought Chuff as he turned through the Syke archway. "He was always busy, and he often sent me on errands. But that's not the same—I don't know——"

He walked into the main office and found all the heads of departments, foremen, and office staff drawn up in a line to greet him. Each in his or her own way offered words of welcome and good wishes.

"Jonathan would deduce their characters from this, I expect," he thought sardonically, observing in spite of himself how one was pompous, another tongue-tied, a third fluent, another nervously tittering. He had no idea what to say in reply, and merely repeated: "Thanks—thank you," in a rather hoarse and grating tone. As they seemed to be stuck there, unable to get themselves away, even when he had come to the end of the line, it occurred to him to mutter something about: "Grandfather would wish us all to carry on as usual, I am sure," and was relieved to find that with an acquiescent murmur they departed.

"And where do I go from here?" he wondered, stalking through into the inner office.

For the last year or so he had occupied a small table and chair in one corner of this room, not too far from Morcar's large desk, his grandfather often swinging his revolving chair and stretching across to hand him a paper or a pattern. From habit he made towards this familiar corner now. But the sight of the empty chair suddenly brought home to him painfully the fact that he would never see his grandfather again, and he missed him, not as the head of Syke Mills or even as a grandfather, but simply as a person, and he grieved. The big desk was laden with a considerable batch of business correspondence, arranged in neat piles according to subject and urgency. He took a tentative step towards it, but could not bring himself to sit down in Morcar's chair. He was glad he had not done so when he was interrupted at this point by Nathan, who, naming one of their large retail tailoring customers, remarked that their pieces (a considerable number) were due to go out to them tomorrow.

"Surely they're ready?" said Chuff, alarmed.

"They're being baled now," said Nathan with satisfaction. "I was wondering whether they'd like some early, like. This afternoon, you know? Show them we're on the job."

Chuff at once, without thinking, sat down in Morcar's chair and drew the telephone towards him. After some preliminary skirmishing with secretaries—"I ought to have asked Ruth to get him for me," he reflected—he found the voice he knew.

"Henry Morcar, Limited," he said.

"Yes?" said the voice. It sounded cold and preoccupied.

"C. H. F. Morcar here," said Chuff firmly.

"Oh!" said the voice, becoming suddenly much warmer. "May I take this opportunity to express my personal condolences about your grandfather, Mr Morcar—I represented our firm at the funeral, as I daresay you observed. I'm exceedingly sorry. I had a great respect and a strong personal liking for Mr Henry Morcar. He was a great man. A very great loss to the whole textile trade."

"How much longer is this going on?" thought Chuff, anguished. "About your pieces due tomorrow," he said aloud.

"Oh!" said the voice, cooling again. "Aren't they ready?"

"Oh, certainly," said Chuff. "They're baling now. We

just wondered whether you would like a few in advance, this afternoon."

"I don't think so," said the voice in a reflective tone. "No, I hardly think so. All arrangements are made for their reception and allocation tomorrow. They're baled as we asked?"

"Of course," said Chuff, though he had no idea whether this was so. "We shall always comply with your instructions——"

"Good," said the voice coldly.

"Our relations, I hope, will be just as before."

"I hope so indeed," said the voice, and rang off.

Somehow the phrasing of this remark disheartened Chuff; he thought it had a doubtful ring. He went down to the warehouse at once to enquire about the baling, and was greatly relieved to find that it was proceeding according to plan. The warehouse foreman was vexed to find this in question.

"We always follow our instructions in this department, Mr Chuff," he said reproachfully. "Mr Morcar always trusted us to follow our instructions."

"I'm sure you do," said Chuff. "It's just that—naturally— I'm very anxious at present that everything should go well." (How disgusting of me to play on the loss of grandfather in this way, he reflected.)

The foreman, however, was soothed and nodded in agreement, and at this moment their talk was interrupted by the arrival of Ruth in a hurry, who announced that the Mayor of Annotsfield was waiting to see young Mr Morcar.

"Good heavens!" exclaimed Chuff, moving off quickly. "What on earth for?"

The Mayor of Annotsfield was exactly what the irreverent youthful Chuff expected West Riding mayors to be: short, stocky, bald, with a decided West Riding accent. He began by offering condolences about Morcar's death, which by this time were beginning to rasp Chuff's nerves.

"How does the mill feel without him, eh?"

"Empty," barked Chuff.

"Aye! I'll bet it does. And what are you going to do about it?"

"How do you mean?" said Chuff.

"Well, who's going to be your Chairman?"

Chuff, astonished, was silent.

"Or are you, happen, thinking of a merger?" Chuff remaining silent, the Mayor continued: "I'm a Yorkshire-man, and I believe in putting my cards on the table. You hold the controlling majority of Syke shares, I make no doubt. Harry will have tied it all up safe. Mergers is all the trend nowadays. Of course I don't pretend my firm is any-thing like Harry Morcar's—whose is? But it's reputable and prospering—as far as anything can prosper under this government—and I think we should do well together. My son's double your age; you wouldn't clash. How do you feel about a merger betwixt us, eh?"

"No," said Chuff.

"You've got other plans in mind. Well, that's that, then," said the Mayor, rising. "You don't mind my mentioning it, do you? No harm done, eh?"

"None."

The Mayor offered his hand. Chuff took it. "Now, take care, young man," said the Mayor. "You've a huge property here. And the goodwill and all. The reputation. Harry's cloths were known all over the world. Don't you go and throw it all away. Consult your accountants at every step. And get a good merchant banker to look after it all for you. Can't do a merger proper, like, without a merchant banker. You're young, you know, lad, and not brought up in this county."

"I'm Yorkshire by birth on both sides," blurted Chuff indignantly.

"I'm right glad to hear you say so, my boy," said the Mayor heartily.

"And I took the full five-year course in textiles at Annotsfield Tech."

"Good, good. Now we'll keep this just between ourselves?"

"Yes, of course."

"Well, then, goodbye and good luck to you."

He went on shaking Chuff's hand until the young man feared he would never get free. At last, however, he managed to open the office door with his left hand, and the Mayor took the hint and went out.

In the main office Chuff was surprised to see Nat Armitage sitting upright on a stiff office chair, rather markedly not talking to anybody. He rose as the Mayor entered and, bowing his head slightly in greeting murmured: "Mr Mayor," in a manner indicative of genuine though mild respect for the first citizen of the borough. The Mayor returned: "Mr Armitage," in what seemed to Chuff a rather sardonic tone, and passed on. Behind his back Nat made what seemed to be signals to Chuff, raising his eyebrows, moving his head towards the outer door, and so on. Not understanding what all this was about, Chuff stood still and made no move, whereupon Nat went forward, opened the door for the Mayor, conducted him down the steps and saw him into his car—which was not, Chuff observed, the official Annotsfield vehicle. Returning—he ran blithely up the steps; for his age he was in pretty good shape, reflected Chuff—Nat took Chuff by the arm, walked him briskly into the inner office and closed the door.

"I wanted to have a serious talk with you, Chuff," he said, seating himself.

"Go ahead."

"Have you fixed a date yet for an extraordinary general meeting of Henry Morcar shareholders?"

"No. Do we need one soon?"

"Well, you'll have to elect a new Chairman. It could be done in the first place by the Board of Directors, and confirmed by the shareholders, I expect. Who are your Directors, by the way?"

"I've met them and I know their names, but I don't remember them—they aren't anybody to matter much," said Chuff uneasily. "I'm one myself, by the way."

"Yes, I expected you would be. Mr Morcar floated when he bought Daisy Mill, I expect."

"I believe so," lied Chuff, who only vaguely remembered what Morcar had told him of the finances of the company, for they did not interest him. He was not without sense, however, and though he had never heard the expression *floated* used in this way before, he guessed at once what it meant.

"Who are you thinking of for Chairman?"

"Can't I be Chairman?" blurted Chuff.

"You could, of course. You own the controlling majority of shares, or rather you will do when the will's probated; you can do pretty much what you like. But I must tell you I think it could be unwise, Chuff. You're very young, and you weren't brought up in the West Riding."

"The Mayor said that. I'm Yorkshire by birth on both sides," said Chuff. Anger drove him beyond politeness; he blurted loudly: "Are *you* wanting to be Chairman, then?"

"Yes," said Nat coolly.

"And where would I come in, then?" shouted Chuff.

"You'd be Managing Director, of course."

"Perhaps you'd like a merger, eh?"

"I couldn't honestly advise that," said Nat. "I couldn't

raise the huge sum necessary to buy out your shareholders—
how many have you, by the way?—and I see no reason why
you should want to buy out the Armitage firm."

"Neither do I," said Chuff brutally. He longed with all his
heart to utter aloud what Morcar had often said to him:
"Armitages have had their day," but managed to hold it in.

Nat coloured slightly, but did not move in his chair.
"You've certainly got enough on your plate without adding
any more," he said calmly. "Don't decide now, Chuff; think
it over; consult your accountants and so on. I would buy
Jennifer's shares to qualify, if you agreed."

Chuff, arriving home for lunch, daunted by these immense
and dangerous prospects of unknown financial territories
which lay ahead of him, found Jonathan working peacefully
over some papers—"lesson notes", he said—in the summer-
house, Susie sitting silent beside him.

"Easy for them," he thought.

"A difficult morning?" suggested Jonathan, as Chuff
slumped on to the bench.

"Nat Armitage proposes he should be Chairman of Henry
Morcar Limited and I should be Managing Director," he
blurted.

"Cool."

"Damned cool."

"But it might not be a bad idea," said Jonathan thoughtfully. "The West Riding might like it. Armitages still have a
great name. You're . . ."

"—young and haven't been brought up in Yorkshire,"
concluded Chuff savagely.

"Still, you're West Riding by birth on both sides."

"Thank you for those kind words."

"What had you thought, yourself, of doing?"

"I hadn't thought," said Chuff. The truth was he had
simply assumed that Syke Mills and its subsidiaries were now

his to do as he liked with; Chairmen, Boards of Directors and so on had not entered his calculations. "What do you think about it all, Jonathan? Seriously?"

"It's too much for you to manage alone, Chuff—yet," said Jonathan gravely.

"You'd like me to go in for a merger, perhaps?"

"Mergers are all the trend. Uncle Harry considered a merger, after all."

"I don't want a merger," said Chuff, biting off each word.

"You'll have to elect a new Chairman to replace Uncle Harry, anyway."

"Armitages have had their day. They're out of date."

"But you are not. You would balance Uncle Nat." (He had settled on this mode of naming his mother's husband.) "Uncle Nat is an honourable man."

"Oh, agreed."

"Then later you can become Chairman. It would all be in the family—you'd all be on the same side."

"Ha!" said Chuff with extreme scepticism. "Families!"

The necessary notices were, however, sent out, the necessary adjustments made to voting shares; Nat Armitage became Chairman of Henry Morcar, Limited, and C. H. F. Morcar its Managing Director. As Jonathan had pro-phesied, the West Riding seemed to approve, and even Chuff admitted that the former Major Armitage was sometimes useful. He knew how to preside at meetings and take votes and things of that kind, so that shareholders who arrived looking rather anxious departed looking soothed. Above all, he did not interfere in the day-to-day working of the mills. Nevertheless, C. H. F. Morcar, though he soon settled, he thought, into his managerial duties, did not forget the fearful blow to his pride which he had received on the first morning of his new career. He did not forget, and he did not intend to do so.

7

SUSIE

CHUFF'S DECISION TO marry in the spring, announced in the New Year, was well received by all concerned except Susie.

Chuff did not notice his sister's reaction at first. When on a couple of nights she slipped off to bed immediately after their evening meal together, he attributed this to natural causes. In any case his evenings nowadays were devoted either to Ruth or to vigorous wrestles with Henry Morcar Limited problems. But after a few more nights he began to notice her absence.

"Where's Susie, Mrs Jessopp?" he enquired.

Mrs Jessopp pursed her lips.

"She's upstairs in her room."

"Has she gone to bed? Is she ill or something?"

Mrs Jessopp hesitated. "I don't think she's ill, exactly," she said. "She seems unhappy."

Chuff threw down the evening *Recorder* and ran upstairs. His knock at Susie's door receiving no reply, he opened the door and burst in. The room was in darkness, but there seemed to be no one in the bed; screwing up his eyes, he thought he perceived a deepened shadow in an armchair.

"Susie!" he said.

The shadow moved.

"Susie, why are you upstairs here in the cold?" he said in his most soothing, loving tone. "Come down and sit with me, lovey, do."

"You don't want me," said Susie.

"What are you talking about? Of course I do. You're my sister."

"If you don't want Jonathan, you don't want me."

"Jonathan's away in Ormbury," said Chuff, puzzled.

"You turned him out."

"I turned Jonathan out!" exclaimed Chuff in capital letters. "What rubbish! I did nothing of the sort! I told him he was always welcome at Stanney Royd."

"That's not the same as asking him to stay here."

Chuff sighed and did not know what to say; he supposed she was right. "Do try to be happy, now you've left school," he produced at last.

"I don't want to stay here when you're married," went on Susie in her obstinate little voice.

"But why not?" said Chuff, dismayed. "Ruth is fond of you."

"Oh, Ruth's all right. But if you think I shall enjoy it, alone here, watching you and Ruth being married, you're mistaken."

That his little sister should know enough of the facts of life to make such a remark was painful to Chuff.

"Why shouldn't Jonathan and I get married?"

"You're too young yet, dear."

"I'm eighteen next birthday."

"Are you really?" said Chuff, astonished. "The years slip by."

"If Jonathan and I can't get married when you do, then I want to go to London and take my L.R.A.M."

"What's that?"

"A music degree," said Susie impatiently.

"Susie, you can't do that."

"Yes, I can."

"No! I shall not allow you to go and live in London alone, Susie," said Chuff firmly, "so you can stop thinking about it."

With this return to normal feeling he realised he could put the light on; he stepped back and did so. Susie was revealed gazing at him pitifully, wan and tear-stained, her lovely eyes large with anguish, her exquisite pale hair dishevelled. Susie's beauty was quite out of the ordinary and few could resist it; her brother was not one of them.

"Ah, Susie!" he said weakly. "I shouldn't have a moment's peace if you were alone in London."

"But what about me?" said Susie in a trembling tone. "You should help me, Chuff."

"What can I do?" said the perplexed Chuff.

"You can ask Jonathan," wailed Susie.

Chuff groaned.

"Put the light out when you go," said Susie.

"I shall do nothing of the kind. Come downstairs to the fire, like a sensible girl."

"No."

"But why not, lovey?"

"I don't want to."

To this there was nothing to be said. Chuff turned on the electric radiator, left the light on, and withdrew. After some agonised indecision, he rang up Jonathan, who sounded cheerful and animated.

"Chuff? I was just about to call you," said Jonathan. "I wanted your advice."

"That's new, from you," growled Chuff.

It appeared that Jonathan had been offered a post as assistant lecturer in English literature in one of the new northern universities, to take effect next autumn.

"That should suit you better than the hurly-burly of school," said Chuff.

"Oh, there'll be plenty of hurly-burly, I don't doubt," said Jonathan cheerfully. "But the place is new and *growing*. Mostly humps of soil and piles of bricks at present, I gather. A lot of organising to do. I should like that, you know."

"I'll bet you would," thought Chuff with the irritated

fondness he usually felt for his half-cousin. "What's the difficulty, then?"

"Ought I to leave Ormbury so soon? It might leave them in a bit of a hole. It seems rather mean to leave so soon? There's a great shortage of teachers, you know. What do you think, Chuff? Seriously?"

Any other person, Chuff would have frankly advised to consult his own advantage, but he knew that this was the way to spur Jonathan in the opposite direction. So he said gravely: "I should think a new university's need is greater."

"Do you think so? Really?" said Jonathan, as delighted as a child.

He *is* a child, thought Chuff, contemptuous yet admiring; he's a good fellow after all, but it's so easy to fool him, I did it nicely that time.

"Look, I want to have a word with you about Susie," he said.

"Is anything wrong?" said Jonathan quickly.

"Well—could you come up for the weekend?" suggested Chuff, finding himself unable to go into a question of such delicacy as marriage, on the telephone. It occurred to him that Jonathan might fear that Susie was changing her affections, so he added hastily: "Susie would be *very* glad to see you."

"I'll come up on Friday night," said Jonathan.

"Good. I'll meet you."

Susie, radiant in a very short new frock of white wool, threw herself into Jonathan's arms the moment he entered Stanney Royd. Clasping her arms about his neck, she then broke into wild tears.

"Why, Susie! What's the matter? Susie! My darling," exclaimed Jonathan fondly. Leading her to a wooden bench which stood in the hall, he seated her and sat beside her, stroking her hair and pressing her face against his shoulders. "What is wrong? Pussy," he murmured in her ear,

Chuff, who found this name of endearment distastefully sentimental, moved impatiently.

"She wants to go to London and live in lodgings and take a musical degree," he said in a loud practical tone.

"Impossible," interjected Jonathan.

"She doesn't want to live with Ruth and me when we're married."

"But it won't be for long. *We* shall be married soon, Susie," said Jonathan.

Susie lifted her head and gazed imploringly at her brother. Chuff, crimson and choking, managed to get out:

"She would like it to be now."

"Why not?" cried Jonathan happily. "That's the best solution—we'll have a double wedding in the Easter holidays. Ormbury isn't too brilliant, but that would only be for one term; then at Lorimer we could have a flat, or a nice little house in the suburbs. Susie will be eighteen in March, you know, Chuff."

His whole person radiated joy. Chuff for his part was excruciatingly torn between relief and shame. He felt with immense relief that his sister's happiness was secure, but at the same time shame that he had placed on Jonathan's shoulders a wife who, however beautiful, would always be a responsibility, perhaps even a drag, rather than a helpmeet and a safeguard. As the two men sat together that night discussing details of the proposed wedding, Chuff wondered whether Jonathan knew this too. Looking at Jonathan's austere profile, Chuff believed that yes, he knew.

II

JONATHAN

1

HONEYMOON

JONATHAN INDEED KNEW. But he undertook the responsibility of Susie not only with deep tenderness but with awestruck joy; to him it was glorious, as a man feels on appointment to a vice-chancellorship or high political office. His only uncertainty was whether he would be equal to the noble task, be worthy of the great responsibility so honourably assigned to him. His thought as he stood beside Susie at the altar was a determination to be, indeed, worthy of his young wife; never in any way to fail her.

The double wedding was performed in fine conventional style in Marthwaite Church. Jonathan had suggested a quiet ceremony, even tentatively hinting at a registrar's office, but Chuff had put his foot down scornfully on this notion, and Jonathan yielded, admitting to himself with amusement that he would enjoy seeing Susie in white satin and lace, and hearing with her the words of the Anglican wedding service—which, when studying it carefully beforehand, he discovered to be gravely beautiful. G. B. Mellor, very spruce and upright, with pugnacious chin protruding firmly, as Ruth's brother of course "gave her away"; Nat Armitage, lean and distinguished with his slight limp, did the same for Susie.

The amount of obstinacy, sheer strength of will, clustered round the vicar in Marthwaite Church was enough to blow the ancient roof off, thought Jonathan, smiling to himself. Chuff and G.B., equally determined to make their way, but in conflicting directions, he thought. (G.B. had made great strides in the Trade Union world lately, he understood; he had become secretary to his union, and though it was only a small one this election pointed the way to higher things.) Jonathan himself was determined on his own ideas, though these were for peace and brotherhood; Nat Armitage, though rather worn and exhausted, yet had the habit of authority. Ruth with her sparkling dark grey eyes and rosy complexion, her strong arms and slightly buxom figure, was the model of a lively, robust and faithful wife who would stand no nonsense from anything which threatened her husband and children. Only his lovely Susie—whose beauty was so outstanding that as she glided gracefully down the aisle there really was a slight movement, a very slight murmur, of appreciation from the assembled guests—looked passive, accepting, with malice towards none; the type of all those in the world who suffered helplessly the persecution of the strong. She looked rather frightened now, observed Jonathan with pity, and as though her bouquet of lilies and white roses would slip from her grasp. (The two brides were dressed alike and carried similar flowers, but whereas Ruth appeared an honest, good, comely young woman, agreeably clad, on whom one could congratulate her husband as a thoroughly sensible and honourable choice, Susie seemed a transcendent figure in, say, a pre-Raphaelite picture; her lustrous pale gold hair came certainly from the brush of Rossetti.) The two grooms rose to welcome their brides. Susie's eyes met Jonathan's; at once those great dark-blue orbs brightened into happiness and she smiled. Jonathan's heart turned over with love.

Chuff and Ruth spent their honeymoon in the Scottish Highlands, Jonathan and Susie in Italy.

Jonathan observed with interest that whereas Chuff had none of old Mrs Morcar's artistic talent—which, passed on to her son, had led him to his textile triumphs—Susie had inherited it in abundance. Not a creator, she had a true appreciative gift; she understood and revelled in Italy's artistic wealth with a just discrimination. She thought Venice a fairyland, Florence a most beautiful city. She smiled with loving glee when confronted with a Carpaccio, thought Titian cross and Raphael boring, though respecting their consummate techniques, adored Michelangelo, but when she occasionally met a Rubens strayed from his native land frowned and said his women were "bulgy".

"Daddy fought in Italy," she remarked once wistfully as they journeyed across the Apennines.

Jonathan gave her a look of sympathy but said nothing: he dared not venture upon this subject, Susie's holy of holies, he knew too well the anguish caused her by her father's violent death.

She had a most sensitive understanding of other people's feelings. To Jonathan this was something of a surprise; she had often seemed, not selfish, but wrapped in a soft silk cocoon of not wishing to intrude. But this was a mistake. For example, she said to him one day suddenly:

"Do you remember the china lamb I gave to grandfather?"

"I do indeed."

"Should you mind if I gave it to Chuff? He might be hurt if I took it away."

Jonathan forebore to tell her that the charming model of the lamb had become Chuff's by inheritance, but choosing his words carefully, urged her to tell her brother that she was glad he kept the lamb on his desk; she wanted him to have it there. At this Susie gave her radiant smile.

The susceptible Italians, beaming fondly, called her *bellissima* and *elegantissima*. Both epithets were true. There was absolutely no vulgarity of any kind in Susie's speech or look or thought, and her appointments of dress and lingerie were exquisite; she made no fuss, but chose unerringly. Sometimes on an impulse she put up her hair; it seemed to fall at once into those wonderful waves and curls one saw in advertisements in glossy magazines. But she soon took it down; Jonathan surmised she found the elaborate dressing artificial, excessive.

Not only was their marriage one of true minds; their sexual relations were an ecstasy. Jonathan had been almost afraid to attempt intercourse, but her surrender was complete and joyous. Her intense happiness made his.

2

MARRIED LIFE

AFTER THIS DELICIOUS Italian dream, Ormbury looked
peculiarly grim. A Midlands industrial town, it had not even
the grace of being their native Yorkshire to console them.
The traffic's volume was appalling, the buildings were ugly
and smoke-grimed; it was useless for Jonathan to make plans
at school for the future, since he would stay only the present
term there. His school colleagues were at first a trifle miffed
at Jonathan's early departure to what they called sardonically higher spheres; dedicated teachers all, they thought the
children deserved the best and most skilful teaching available
and it was the duty of an intelligent, enthusiastic young man
like Jonathan to help provide it. But when they saw Susie
they gasped and adopted a different attitude. With the
exception of one or two female teachers who had hoped to
win Jonathan for themselves, they treated Susie with great
solicitude, lowering their voices and using their best language
when they spoke to her, and asking Jonathan with much
diffidence whether she wished to come to school sports and
entertainments—compulsory for them, such a beauty as
Susie's set her free to choose for herself. Susie smiled and
listened and asked questions, apparently rather naïve but on
further consideration rather deep. She attended classes in
tapestry work at the local technical college and began to take
great interest in this needlework.

Jonathan's landlady, an honest but rather sharp-tongued
dame, underwent a similar conversion. Not too pleased when
Jonathan had informed her of his coming marriage and asked
her to allow him to bring his wife to the lodgings, when Susie

arrived she gaped at her, and then immediately took her under her wing. Discovering that the young wife knew nothing of housekeeping—how should she? Her childhood had been spent waited on by African servants, her teens under the highly competent dominion of Jennifer and Mrs Jessopp —she undertook to instruct her in cookery. Susie was earnest about this but rather slow; the poor child did not even know how to boil a potato, as the landlady exclaimed commiseratingly to Jonathan. At last, however, one day an apple pie was placed on the table, and Susie, flushed and excited, admitted that she had made it. The pie was really good and Jonathan said so emphatically; thenceforward apple pies appeared on the menu rather often, perhaps, but Jonathan always brought a keen appetite to them. Since Susie's happiness was the greatest aim of his life, when Susie was happy he was happy too.

3

FINANCE

He was considerably distressed, therefore, when one day Susie expressed dissatisfaction. The item concerned was their car. She was learning to drive, and one evening she observed casually that her tutor thought it would be better if she waited till she had acquired her new car before continuing her lessons.

"We aren't going to have a new car," said Jonathan, treating this as the sales talk which in fact it was.

"Why not?" said Susie mildly. "He says ours is out of date, and the gears and gadgets of a modern car would be different and confuse me."

The adjective *modern* struck Jonathan as insulting in this connection. He reflected on the age of the car. It was, he remembered, the same car that Morcar had presented to the cousins quite a number of years ago. Chuff had sold his half of it to Jonathan for an almost nominal sum, as soon as he had saved enough from his Syke Mill earnings to buy one for himself. To travel on his honeymoon he had bought another, large, powerful and handsome; but that of course belonged to a different era, when he had become his grandfather's heir and Managing Director of the mills. Still perhaps Jonathan's car was a trifle antique. He said nevertheless:

"Cars are expensive, and we shall need a good deal of money to set us up in Lorimer, you know. Furniture and things of that kind. And we may want to buy a house."

"But I have a lot of money," said Susie, happily. "A big cheque came only this morning from Syke Mill."

Jonathan, who of course was incapable of inspecting or enquiring about Susie's correspondence or the bank account he had established for her, was silent.

"Don't you want me to have a lot of money?" said Susie with her customary directness.

Jonathan hesitated. "I would rather we lived on what I earned," he said. "I don't believe in unearned incomes. Everyone should have what they earn, what they deserve for their services to the community."

Susie's brightness slightly dimmed.

"Grandfather wanted me to have his money," she said.

This was true, and Jonathan felt genuinely perplexed. Had he the right to deprive Susie of the enjoyments willed to her (and indeed to her through him) by Harry Morcar? He sighed.

"I don't think it's kind to deprive grandfather of his wishes just because he's dead, and can't stand up for himself," said Susie.

"He doesn't know, my darling."

"That makes it worse," said Susie gravely.

Jonathan smiled, but the smile was awry. If there had been the slightest tincture of greed in Susie's utterance he would have seen the car project as a vulgar capitalist selfishness, but her eagerness was completely innocent, childlike. He wrestled with the problem all night, and in the morning, incapable of denying Susie something so reasonable, bought a modest car. The low price he obtained for the old one supported the salesman's contention that a new one was overdue, and he felt relieved by this justification.

"If we keep Uncle Harry's money we must give a lot of it away," he said to Susie.

"Of course," agreed Susie cheerfully.

4

UNIVERSITY

THE CAR CERTAINLY proved useful when they moved to Lorimer.

From the first they were exceedingly happy there. The city was northern, and full of those multifarious democratic societies which the north loves. They joined several, and enjoyed this widening of scope. The faculty surveyed Susie's beauty with a kindly but serious air; they had a more discerning eye than persons met hitherto, and seemed to perceive that certain disadvantages might accompany this very unusual personal allure.

At the University the Vice-Chancellor was experienced and able, his wife intelligent and friendly; Jonathan's professor, notable in his field, though outwardly stern was one of the kindest and most honourable men of letters he had known; there were, of course, a few mean and malicious, and a few more merely silly, men and women on the staff, but they were not much in favour and would soon, Jonathan surmised, vanish to scholastically lower though higher-paid positions. Jonathan felt immensely at home in the academic atmosphere. The quiet, urbane, polite speech, where no punches were pulled because words were used in their precise and potent meanings, agreed perfectly with his own inclinations; he enjoyed a feeling of boyish pride when he saw his gown hanging on the wall of his office.

The students were rather startling at first, certainly. Their English was too often poor, their accent ugly; if male they grew on their youthful heads and cheeks more hair than there was room for, and therefore usually looked dirty, as if soap could not penetrate the thicket; if female, they looked the same because their long tangled locks were so disagreeably unkempt. To be careless and slovenly in dress was the fashion, and affectionate demonstrations in public between the sexes ditto. But on all this Jonathan turned a forgiving and affectionate eye; their young faces were so eager, their ideals (though often vague and unpractical) so noble; their ignorance so touching. After a few test questions, meant to be awkward and designed to ascertain his views, they seemed to decide to like him; on his side he tried to handle their touchy adolescent egos with sympathetic and scrupulous care.

In his work he was indeed happy. He was allotted a course of first-year lectures on English novelists of the nineteenth century. This was a great pleasure, in fact, as he said to Susie, just his cup of tea. He rebuked himself sometimes for venturing to imagine that he lectured well, but in fact results showed that this was the case. Returning students' essays, too, was a task he welcomed; he longed so earnestly to assist the struggling lad or girl in front of him to express their ideas, however banal these might be, that these sessions were always full of interest to him. Where he felt less certain was in his tutorial classes. He found that the student to whom a question was addressed either went on so boringly long that the discussion which was the object of the exercise never got under way, or replied in so scanty a fashion that no fruitful point emerged for discussion. In either of these conditions, Jonathan was not perhaps as yet quite formidable enough to command the attention of ten or dozen students not much younger than himself; they grew restless, and interest in members of the other sex who were present crept in. Confessing this difficulty to his professor, he found that it was a common one and received some useful hints on control; he struggled and, he hoped, improved. On the whole he felt he was doing useful work, and rejoiced.

As regards housing accommodation, Jonathan and Susie were fortunate. In the summer vacation, before term claimed Jonathan, they found an old, indeed almost decrepit, cottage on one of the pleasanter roads leading out of the city, and spent a good deal, which nevertheless the result justified, in restoring it to full and agreeable use. White-painted, with the garden tidied to reveal bright country flowers (yellow and crimson and golden) the outside was charming, and Susie showed great skill in making the interior equally attractive. Jonathan, who knew his mother's skill in this respect, once suggested that she should be consulted, but Susie replied simply:

"I want to do it myself, Jonathan."

There was no more to be said. The young Oldroyds visited house sales and antique shops, and Old Cottage was admired and frequently visited by faculty and students alike, for Susie's musical evenings were both respected and enjoyed.

Summer faded into autumn and sharpened into winter. Wood fires crackled warmly on the huge old hearth; Susie bent over her tapestry, Jonathan read to her or talked about his students. They discussed modern novels and plays without alarm, and were happy in agreement. When they found that Susie was with child, their happiness became complete.

III

CHUFF

1

DESIGNER

RETURNING FROM HIS honeymoon, Chuff entered Syke Mill whistling cheerfully. The new car had coped smoothly with the gradients of the Highlands, of which the scenery was certainly striking, his wife proved all that he desired, and his own performance had been decidedly satisfactory. The Syke order book was full, running on the patterns Morcar had prepared the previous year, and no crashing error seemed to have been made in the three mills during his absence.

But all too soon this content was dimmed. Nat Armitage rang up to welcome him home and pleasantly told him of one or two points on which Syke Mill had consulted him during its managing director's absence. Chuff, though vexed, thanked him energetically, and by this means contrived to indicate that it was unnecessarily good of a non-executive Chairman to interest himself so keenly in the mill affairs.

"And how's your pattern range coming on?" pursued Nat.

"I'm just going up to the design department now," said Chuff—a remark intended to call forth the answer he received.

"I won't keep you, then," said Nat hastily.

Chuff found the design department depressing. Its head, a long thin lean bald elderly man in spectacles named Simmonds, was no doubt extremely reliable and had perfect textile taste, but could never conceive a design which would sweep the market. The two younger men, and even the run-and-fetch boy, had the same air of uncreative loyalty; a woman in the thirties, whose eyes held a spark of revolt, was engaged with colour ranges of yarn and seemed to know her

job, but the whole department seemed quiet, passive, remote
from life's hurly-burly, almost as if lying on a dusty shelf,
waiting of course, thought Chuff crossly, for Morcar to rush
in with an idea to startle them into hectic activity. The
months which had passed since his grandfather's death had
not diminished his personal grief, but perhaps pushed it into
a more distant corner of his heart, and his present reaction
was to feel vexed with Morcar.

"What on earth was he about, falling and letting himself
get killed like that?" he thought irritably.

It was delightful, however, to return home to lunch in his
own house, with his own wife at the corner of his own table,
and eat viands prepared for his satisfaction alone.

"You look worried, Chuff," said Ruth, solicitous. "Of
course there'll be many problems waiting for you; they'll
have missed you while you've been away."

"Yes, and Miss Sprott isn't a patch on her predecessor,"
said Chuff smiling. (Miss Sprott, a very maiden lady in the
forties, was Ruth's successor as Chuff's personal secretary, in
reality a very good one, as the sensible Ruth at once remarked.) "Well—I'm worried about the Design Department,
as a matter of fact. I don't think much of Simmonds."

"Technically he's perfect," said Ruth.

"Oh, I daresay. But he won't set the Thames on fire."

"Perhaps not."

"Grandfather did."

"Yes, indeed," agreed Ruth with fervour.

"I must get somebody new there," decided Chuff. "It's no
use to keep putting it off. I must *do* something. But how you find
a brilliant new designer, I don't know. New and young."

"Mr Morcar came out of the Annotsfield Tech—and so
did you."

"True."

"You might go and see the Principal."

"Oh, lord!" said Chuff ruefully. "He didn't think much of *me*, I'm afraid."

"It's different now," said Ruth, soothing.

A few evenings later, therefore, Chuff, feeling uncomfortably like the merely average student he had always been at the Tech, was ushered in to see the Principal, who gave him a grin showing complete awareness of their former and present situations.

"I was deeply grieved by your grandfather's death," he said. "Mr Morcar was a man of great skill in his craft, and of massive integrity—also extremely lovable."

"Yes," agreed Chuff, nonetheless wishing that these tributes, which seemed to condemn him by comparison, would cease. "I want a young designer," he blurted.

"Ah. For the present or the future?"

"Well, of course I should like both," said Chuff honestly. "But—well, I don't know. I have an elderly man whose technique is perfect. I want someone with new ideas. But not too young, you see, or he won't have any influence. If you see what I mean."

"And you have come to see me?" said the Principal in an interrogative tone.

"I hoped you would find me one," blurted Chuff.

"Mr Morcar," said the Principal, suddenly becoming very stiff: "You are perhaps not aware that we never recommend students to textile firms. Most of our students come on Day Release *from* textile firms where they are apprentices. I am sure you will understand that we could not suggest to these students that they should leave their present employers."

"Oh, quite—of course not," said Chuff, flurried.

"All we do—or could do—would be to place an announcement of the job on our notice board."

"I might as well advertise it in the *Annotsfield Recorder*."

"You could do that, of course."

"I don't want to do that," said Chuff, vexed. "I don't want to tell the whole West Riding that Morcars need a new designer."

"I see your point. These lads," went on the Principal after a pause, "range from sixteen to twenty-one, you know."

"That's rather young for my purpose."

"It's a five-year course."

"I know your textile course," said Chuff grimly. "I took it."

"So you did. Well, it just occurs to me that we have a young man, a part-time teacher, who might suit you. He teaches here one evening a week, and for the rest of the time is a free-lance designer. Carpets, curtains, fabrics of all kinds, I believe."

"That's not textile design in my sense of the word."

"Agreed. But he has had a thorough textile training. He's taken his City and Guilds examination—he won a medal—he knows the new man-made fibres—and I believe he has a real flair. Or so the head of the department tells me. He teaches both weaving mechanism and design. As he teaches here only one night a week, it seems to me he could do your job without interference with his work here."

"How old?"

"About twenty-five, I imagine."

"He sounds hopeful," said Chuff, beginning to congratulate himself on his clever discovery. "Is he an Annotsfield man?"

"No. West of England."

"Ah. Smooth broadcloth. High quality cloth. Why is he up here, then?"

"I don't know. He's married. His wife is an artist, and he too paints, I believe, in his spare time."

"Well," said Chuff very cheerfully: "He sounds just the ticket."

"Would you like to see him?"

"Yes."

"Shall I send for him? He's teaching tonight."

"Well, no," said Chuff, wriggling. "That's a little too, too——"

"You don't want to commit yourself."

"Not yet."

"Shall we go round the textile department together, then? And come across him *en route*?"

Chuff agreed gratefully, and the two men went down to the basement in the lift.

"This is Mr Paul Yarrow," said the Principal, leading Chuff to a young man who, standing by a squared blackboard on which was inscribed in coloured chalks an embryonic textile design, was evidently discoursing about it to a dozen or so lads in desks in front of him. "Ah, a stripe, I see."

"I don't much care for stripes," said Chuff, without thinking. (He had grown to detest stripes ever since he had learned to perceive what an awful striped suit he had been wearing when he first landed in England—what his grandfather must have thought of it!) "That is, if they're too obtrusive," he added hastily.

"I never made a stripe more than half an inch wide," said Yarrow in a resentful tone. His accent was what Chuff had learned to label south-country.

"I should hope not indeed," said Chuff. He glanced at the short lengths of yarn which hung over the board. "A good blue," he observed.

"Excuse me, I just want a word with——" began the Principal, turning and hurrying towards the door. "Mr C. H. F. Morcar of Henry Morcar, Limited," he added with a wave of his hand. "You've heard of Morcars, I am sure, Mr Yarrow."

"Oh, yes, indeed," said Yarrow as before.

Chuff looked at him. According to the standards of the day he was well dressed, wearing dark blue corduroy trousers and a white wool jumper with a polo neck. His hair was very dark, glossy and abundant; carefully carelessly arranged in heavy waves which spread over his large white forehead. Sideburns of course, and a beard of course. (Chuff did not like beards; he associated them partly with old Boer farmers, and partly with his maternal great-grandfather, old Mr Shaw, who he always understood had been a pettifogging rascal.) The face, however, was well-shaped; the eyes, dark and large behind their horn spectacles with broad sidepieces, defiant but perhaps honest. He certainly looked "modern". "We took him by surprise, after all," reflected Chuff. It occurred to him that this Yarrow lad might know more about textiles than he did; he had better leave the investigations of his qualifications to Mr Simmonds. "A good blue," he repeated. Yarrow said nothing, rather markedly.

"You've got your City and Guilds, I gather."

Yarrow muttered an affirmative.

"And you're well acquainted with the new man-mades?"

"I am."

"The truth is," said Chuff, extremely embarrassed but also rather proud of himself for this, his first important independent action, "I want a young assistant designer. If the idea interests you, call and see the head of my design department, say tomorrow afternoon."

Yarrow looked astonished, as well he might, by the abruptness of this offer.

"You might bring a few specimens with you, to show Mr Simmonds."

"Can do," said the young man shortly.

Chuff got himself out of the room with a confused mumble. He was crimson and sweating with the effort of decision, but on the whole well satisfied.

"That was a bit sudden, I must say. But the Principal praised him. Well, it's up to Simmonds. If he doesn't like him, he can turn him down. All the same it was a good blue."

Chuff knew enough of textiles to be aware that the apparent goodness of the blue was caused by the colours surrounding it, that is, by Yarrow.

"He's one of these poetic, artistic chaps, like Jonathan," he mused. "But that's what we want, after all. Well, it's up to Simmonds."

2

THE URGE TO MERGE

IT WAS IN the autumn, a few months after Paul Yarrow joined the Design Department of Henry Morcar, Limited, that Miss Sprott, looking nervous and alarmed, handed Chuff a letter on the large new size of notepaper which all business firms seemed to be using nowadays. Miss Sprott very often looked nervous and alarmed, so Chuff did not attach too much importance to her pallor and shaking hand.

Dear Mr. Morcar, he read:

> *It was with the very greatest regret that our group, and I am sure the whole of the wool textile trade, heard of the death of your former Chairman, Mr Henry Morcar, last year. His ability in design was known, not only in this country, but one might almost say, all over the world, and his skill in the selection of materials, machinery and personnel was equally well known. The firm of Henry Morcar Ltd. must feel his loss as a very great deprivation.*

"Tell us something we don't know," said Chuff rudely.

> *It has seemed to my Board that great advantages might accrue if the experience at our disposal were united with the great organisation, and of course the goodwill, built up by your grandfather.*
>
> *In these circumstances I have been authorised by my Board to approach you with a view to offers being made for the whole of the issued share Capital of your Company.*

"What!" shouted Chuff, crimson. "Miss Sprott! Get me Major Armitage on the 'phone."

Association with our group would offer wide opportunities for the development of your Company, and—if I may be permitted to say so—there would in the future be posts of major responsibility within the group for which a man of your age and ability should be well suited.

"Uncle Nat! I've had the most outrageous letter from the Company Secretary of Messrs. Hamsun or some such name——"

"Yes, I've had one from them too."

"Proposing to buy up all our shares."

"The urge to merge. It's the modern trend."

"What on earth are they up to? I never heard such cheek in my life. Who are they, anyway?"

"I believe the original unit was a Lancashire firm——"

"Cotton!" exclaimed Chuff with contempt.

"—but they've merged and merged, and now they're a very large group."

"It's pretty cool, I must say. Grandfather worked all his life building up this business, and now they want to come and take it away, just like that."

"They want to *buy* it," Nat corrected him. "If you sold out at a good price, you could invest the money well and live comfortably, without anxiety."

"And what do I do with the rest of my life?"

"They would no doubt offer you a seat on the Board. That remark about posts of major responsibility means that, I expect."

"And how long would that last? The moment I did anything they didn't approve of, or even wanted to, they'd throw me out on my ear. There are ways and ways."

"It's a possibility which must be remembered," said Nat cautiously.

"Uncle Nat, you want to sell out."

c

"It would be a relief."

"Well, I don't. And let me remind you, I hold the majority of the voting shares."

"I'm aware of it," said Nat drily.

There was a pause.

"Well, what do we do now?" demanded Chuff.

"I think I'd better read you the letter their Chairman has sent to me."

"Go ahead. Though it won't make any difference to my view."

The letter, after making much the same suggestions as the one addressed to Chuff, urged that secrecy should be maintained about the proposal until the matter was further advanced.

After our respective financial advisers have met, I hope you and your colleagues will feel able to give our offer full consideration and that we shall have the opportunity of discussing the matter together personally.

"He's pretty cool, calmly assuming that the matter will go any further. I'll write him a letter of refusal that'll curl his hair."

"You can't do that."

"Why not?"

"It's not ethical conduct, for directors to prevent their shareholders from selling their shares without consulting them."

Chuff felt as though he would burst from rage and frustration.

"What do we do, then?"

"We'd better get ourselves a financial adviser."

"And how do we do that?"

"Our banker will advise us, no doubt."

"Won't he do himself?"

"I think we want a high-up London chap—one of standing and weight."

"Very well—you go ahead and get one. But, Nat, I am not going to give in."

"You may have to change your mind," said Nat, ominous.

3

SOME SHARES

CHUFF AWOKE TO the sound of falling water. He rose from bed and leaned out of the window. Heavy rain was pouring down, the gutters roared, and in the dim pre-dawn light he half saw a strong stream of dirty water rushing down the Stanney Royd drive, dragging the red surface sand with it.

"Is it raining?" asked Ruth from the bed.

"Like hell it is."

"I wish you weren't going by this train," said Ruth wistfully.

Chuff, who had the same superstitious feeling about this early train which his grandfather had so lamentably failed to catch, said obstinately: "It's a good train."

"Is Nat calling for you?"

"No."

"He easily could have done."

"He offered, but I prefer to drive myself, thank you."

There was a silence, in which the sound of water increased.

"I think I'll get up and make a cup of tea," said Ruth, throwing back the bedclothes.

"You'll do nothing of the kind," said Chuff. He spoke sharply, for Ruth was pregnant and needed consideration.

"Don't be so cross, Chuff," said Ruth. "You're always snapping at me nowadays."

"I'm sorry, love," said Chuff, returning to the bed and taking her gently in his arms. "But this interview today is very important—you might even call it fateful."

"I know," said Ruth, stroking his cheek.

The Chairman and Managing Director of Henry Morcar,

Limited, caught the London train without damage, though even in the short transit from car park to station, they became uncomfortably wet.

"Hell of a day," said Chuff.

"I hope Syke Mill has no chinks to let water through," said Nat.

"It hasn't, nor Daisy either, but I'm not so sure about Old Mill."

"I wonder you still cling to that old place, Chuff," said Nat irritably. "It's more bother than it's worth."

"That's your view."

"It is."

"It's not mine."

"Your view is never mine."

"Why should it be? I've a right to my own view."

"If you're going to conduct this interview in this mood, Chuff, we might as well turn round and go home."

"That's what you'd like, isn't it? You want to sell out. You've no faith in me. You don't think me capable of running Syke."

"You're young, and it's a great responsiblity. There is Susie to think of, you know."

"You mean Jonathan, don't you?"

"I resent your tone to me, Morcar," said Nat angrily. "I'm twice your age and have infinitely more experience, and I'm giving up a great deal of time which I would prefer to devote to my own firm, to try to help you. I think I deserve a better response than to be accused of favouring my wife's son, who in any case is your brother-in-law and half-cousin."

It was the first time Nat had addressed him formally by his surname, and Chuff could not help a twinge of pleasure at thus having manhood as it were conferred upon him. He replied brusquely, however:

"I resent your obvious desire to sell out."

"I don't conceal my belief that it would be the wise thing to do, for the sake of the whole family."

"We're going round in circles. I disagree."

"Their offer includes a seat for you on the group Board."

"They'd chuck me out as soon as they'd pinched all I know."

"Your bargain with them would include a sizeable holding of the Hamsun stock, of course," said Nat impatiently.

"There are ways of pushing a man out, I expect, irrespective of voting power."

"Of course you'd have to prove your worth and make a fight for it."

"Do you think I wouldn't?" said Chuff, grinding his teeth.

"Oh, you'd fight for it," said Nat sardonically.

At this point the steward came down the car, offering tea and coffee.

"Well, now that we've demonstrated once again the complete disunity of our Board, let's have breakfast,'" said Nat.

In spite of themselves the two men grew friendlier as they ate the hot food.

"Why can't we just tell these chaps *No*, and forget about it?" said Chuff.

"I've told you over and over again. It wouldn't be ethical to our shareholders. We've got to tell them of the offer. We can't deprive them of the chance of making a lot of money, without consulting them."

"You keep saying this without explaining it. How will they make a lot of money?"

"They'll be offered a high price for their Henry Morcar shares."

"I see. And is this ethical idea a general view in business?"

"Of course. We have a responsibility to our shareholders."

Chuff was silent till the table was cleared. Then he said: "This was my grandfather's business and I shall fight to retain its independence. Though how one fights in these circumstances, I don't know."

"Alfriston and Howard will tell us."

"Who *are* Alfriston and Howard?" said Chuff impatiently.

"A leading firm of merchant bankers whom we have retained. They will advise us."

"Us?"

"I shall support you."

"You will?" said Chuff, surprised.

"I shall."

"Why?"

"I think it's the right thing to do."

"Well, thanks," said Chuff reluctantly.

"Oh, don't thank me. My aims aren't the same as yours. By putting up a fight we shall get the best price for the shareholders' shares."

"And for our own, of course. Very ethical," said Chuff.

"I'm being perfectly frank and open with you, Morcar, as I have been throughout. You'll admit that, perhaps."

"Oh, I do."

"There's no need for us to quarrel personally."

"I don't think I can help it," said Chuff.

Nat laughed, and in spite of himself Chuff gave a grim smile.

"We're on the same side, Chuff, and must fight the battle together, up to a point."

"What point?"

"They may make an offer so large that no one in his senses would refuse it. In that case our shareholders will sell. Hamsun's will buy; heavily equipped with shares they will demand seats on the Board and be a perpetual nuisance there. In that case, better to sell out completely and let them take over."

Chuff looked his Chairman in the eye. "Never," he said.

The building which housed Messrs Alfriston and Howard was a fine one; post-war, of an austere elegance. Its furnishings were highly expensive but quietly tasteful.

"Jonathan would like this," thought Chuff wistfully.

They were ushered into the presence of Messrs Alfriston and Howard. Howard was short and dark. Alfriston taller and fair. Their dark city suits were of such excellence that Chuff at once decided to change this tailor. He had been prepared to dislike them as smooth city slickers, and was disconcerted to find his impressions favourable.

After a few preliminaries, in which the two Annotsfield men were courteously greeted—Nat was hailed as Major Armitage, and it suddenly occurred to Chuff that possibly he did not like being addressed as *Nat* by a man so much younger than himself as Chuff, or as Uncle Nat by a non-relative—the four men sat down together, Howard opened a folder which lay in front of him, and they began business.

"We gather that you are not in favour of a merger, Mr Morcar," said the fair Alfriston.

"That's right."

"There are many points in its favour. It would secure you more efficient running, a more economic use of capital, a wider market. Large units are more able to cope with European competition."

"We cope pretty well already," said Chuff with satisfaction.

"We agree there. Henry Morcar Limited is a valuable company."

"Yes—look at our dividends," said Chuff as before.

"Shall we take a look at the whole financial structure?"

said Alfriston. He nodded to the dark Howard, who proceeded to give in a quiet, cool tone every possible financial
detail about Henry Morcar Ltd—its dividends for the past five
years, its capital, its subsidiaries Daisy Mill and Old Mill, its
labour force, its wages bill. In fact, he put forward a great
deal more about Henry Morcar Ltd than Chuff knew himself.

"How did you learn all these details?" he said, trying not
to show his dismay.

"It's a public company—the details are available," said
Alfriston mildly. "In fact, your company is a first-class
proposition, Mr Morcar, and the price per ordinary share
offered by Messrs Hamsun, which we have received from
their financial advisers, is quite unacceptable."

"What is their price?" murmured Nat. (He was looking
pinched and faded, Chuff thought, and it occurred to him
to wonder, not without an unkind pleasure, how Messrs
Armitage would come out of a searching analysis such as
Howard had directed upon the Morcar firm; not too well, he
thought.)

"Twenty-five shillings per ordinary £1 share."

"That's ridiculous," said Nat.

"Quite. Thirty-five would be nearer the mark," said
Howard.

"Still not enough. Particularly as you are not eager for the
transaction," continued Alfriston. "I believe Messrs Hamsun are not looking for a quick bargain; they genuinely wish
for a productive merger."

"They're Lancashire people and know nothing of wool,"
growled Chuff.

"No, no! Their main works are on the fringe of the West
Riding and they have a considerable textile reputation. Our
task is to push them into raising their price to an acceptable
level."

"But what's the good of it all, Mr Alfriston?" said Chuff.

"We have very few shareholders outside the family, and the family do not want a merger. We can vote down any shareholders who desire one—if indeed any do. I appreciate the advantages you mention," he went on, rather pleased with himself for sounding so statesmanlike, "but to me, independence outweighs them all."

There was a pause.

"Mr Morcar," began Alfriston, "how did you first get to know of this proposed merger?"

"By the letter Hamsun's sent me, of course—I sent you a copy," said Chauff, irritated.

"You hadn't noticed any movements in Morcar stock lately?" said Alfriston in his smooth courteous tones. Chuff remaining silent, dumbfounded, he rephrased the question: "The company secretary hasn't reported to you any sizeable number of re-registrations?"

The angry blood rushed to Chuff's face with such force that for a moment his vision blurred. "It's Susie!" he shouted silently to himself. "She's sold some of her shares! Jonathan didn't want any of grandfather's money, I remember. By God, if Jonathan has done this to me, I'll break his damned neck."

He came to himself to find that Nat had touched his arm and was looking at him with concern. Messrs Alfriston and Howard were also directing upon him glances of compassion.

"Then there is your Pension Scheme," proceeded Howard kindly: "I am not sure whether we ascertained that one did exist."

"I think not," mumbled Chuff hoarsely.

"That may perhaps be a good thing in the present situation," pursued Howard. "The Trustees of Pension Schemes often invest their funds in the firm itself, if the firm is a good investment, and thus, you see, they can hold the balance in the voting. I am sure you see the significance of this."

"I see it."

"You will have to convince them particularly, as large shareholders, of whatever course of action you wish to follow."

"I don't think we have a Pensions Scheme," mumbled Chuff again. The ensuing silence convinced him that in fact they had such a scheme, and he cursed the mild elderly clerkish employee who acted as company secretary, for leaving him uninformed on these essential details. He then gathered himself together and made the greatest effort of his life.

"Gentlemen," he said quietly: "As you can see, I am completely ignorant of these financial matters. I have always devoted myself only to the textile side. I shall be grateful if you will instruct me."

At these words the artificial calm of the faces of Messrs Alfriston and Howard relaxed a little, and they spoke a trifle faster and in warmer tones.

"The next move will be Messr⌐ Hamsun's announcement of the proposed merger in the press," said Alfriston.

"The press!" gasped Chuff. Nat seemed beyond speech.

"And various newspaper representatives will, of course, telephone you to obtain your views."

"Oh, no!"

"Oh, don't worry. Put them on to us. Of course you will issue a statement too. As a matter of courtesy, you should write to the Chairman of Hamsun's Board, Major Armitage, presenting your Board's views. No doubt you have already prepared such a letter?"

Nat looked at Chuff, who drew out from his pocketbook a letter he had, in fact, prepared and had had revised by Ruth on the score of grammar. He handed it over to Alfriston, who read it gravely. Chuff held his head down; he felt a burning shame that this amateur, ill-informed document, speaking sentimentally of his grandfather's creation of Henry Morcar, Limited and his own feeling that it would be cowardice on his part to let it go, should pass beneath this cool experienced scrutiny. At length the merchant banker folded the letter and laid it down.

"I'm not sure that this is the wisest line to take, Mr Morcar," he said pleasantly. "For myself I should prefer a statement that your Board is well satisfied with its present independent position and not eager for a merger, and that the price per share offered is of course far too low, quite out of the question. Should you feel that to be a good line to take, Howard?"

"Yes, I think so," said Howard in a considering tone.

"Would you care for me to draft the letter? I should be glad to do so if you wish. One has to be so careful in one's language, or one is apt to be tripped over small legal points."

"I should be grateful if you would guide me by a draft," said poor Chuff.

"Then if Hamsun's pursue the matter, we can say that your Board has determined to beat off this proposed take-over, but realising that they have a duty to the share-holders, are endeavouring to furnish information which would justify Messrs Hamsun in offering a much higher price."

"Yes."

"Of course you are prepared to furnish a forecast of favourable profits next year? More favourable than this year's, I mean?"

"Yes," said Chuff, trying not to blench.

"I am glad of that," said Howard very soberly, "for I had gained rather an impression that you were coasting along at present on your grandfather's achievements."

"We have a new designer," said Chuff boldly, "for whom I personally forecast a great future."

"Good, good."

"You see, Mr Morcar, a more favourable prospect for next year's working will be absolutely essential, because we have the impression—in fact we *know*—that one of the large family blocks of shares on which you are relying, has been broken up and come on to the market."

"This is almost certainly what gave Hamsun the idea of a takeover," said Alfriston, taking up the tale. "A block of shares in this desirable company came on the market, they picked them up, and so are already in an advantageous position."

"So, as we said, you will need to convince your other shareholders that Henry Morcar Limited, is too good an investment to sell out of."

"Of course, Hamsun will probably offer some shares in the new company, in exchange," said Howard quickly.

"Is there any other point you wish to take up?" said Alfriston.

"No—I think we must now digest all you have told us," said Chuff stiffly.

"We must have a Board meeting of Henry Morcar Limited," said Nat.

"Yes. The announcement of the proposed merger will be in the press the day after tomorrow, we are told."

Chuff held his face still, and even forced a smile as the four men shook hands in farewell.

"For God's sake let's get ourselves a drink," said Nat when they were out of the building, seizing Chuff's arm. "I surely need one."

"I have some telephoning to do first," said Chuff, disengaging his arm.

"*Who* has sold their shares?" said Nat.

"Susie, of course. Jonathan put her up to it."

"No!"

"He didn't want grandfather's money. He has these anti-capitalist notions."

"I agree, but he wouldn't do it without telling you."

"That remains to be seen."

In a telephone booth in the marble hall Chuff rang up first the unfortunate Company Secretary.

"Have there been any considerable movements in our share holdings lately, Mr Jenkins?" said Chuff. He tried to keep his tone dry, free from emotion.

"Yes. I have them all listed in preparation for the next Board," babbled Mr Jenkins cheerfully. "Though I expect you have heard of them already from Mrs Oldroyd."

"Oh, they are from my sister's holding?"

"Yes."

"And why didn't you tell me this before?" said Chuff in a quiet but blistering tone.

"Old Mr Morcar used to ask me regularly for a report," began the Secretary, offended.

Chuff slammed down the receiver.

"Is Jonathan there, Susie?" he enquired, when at last he made the connection with Old Cottage.

"No. He's at the University all day today. He'll be home about six," said Susie.

"Susie, have you been selling some of your Henry Morcar shares?"

"Yes," said Susie brightly.

"Why?" said Chuff.

"Jonathan said he didn't want any of grandfather's money," said Susie in her childish tones. "So I sold the shares and bought some others. It's to be a sort of birthday present for him."

Chuff's composure broke, and he raged. "You damned little fool, you've ruined me!" he shouted.

"What? What? Chuff? I didn't hear you properly," cried Susie.

"How did you sell them? Did Jonathan do it for you?"

"No; it's a secret, you see; a surprise for his birthday. He doesn't know anything about it. I just picked a stockbroker from a brass plate in town," said Susie cheerfully.

"Susie, you have ruined me. And Syke Mill, and all of us. You couldn't have done anything which have would hurt Grandfather more."

"Chuff, Chuff!" wailed Susie. "I don't understand."

"Come away, Chuff!" urged Nat at this point, trying to drag the young man out of the booth. "Show some sense, man! Remember her condition!"

Chuff, stupefied with fury, slammed down the receiver and suffered himself to be led away.

The morning's rain had now turned into a damp, heavy fog; the train to the north was exceedingly late, crawling and stopping feebly through the dark counties. The Ire Valley was even foggier than the country south of Annotsfield, and by the time Chuff reached Stanney Royd he was sick with frustration, and as thankful to see Ruth as if he had been travelling for months through a hostile country where nobody spoke his language. Ruth had a meal ready for him, with hot coffee; he tried to eat, but could hardly get anything down; presently he gave up the attempt, and in hoarse tones, with a man's hard tears rolling down his cheeks, began to sob out to his wife the events of the day.

"Oh, poor Susie, poor Susie," grieved Ruth.

"And poor us," said Chuff.

"Oh, I don't think it's as bad as that, Chuff," said Ruth. "If you do have to sell out, you'll have enough to live on, you know."

"I looked such a fool, Ruth. I don't know anything about these finance things."

"How could you? But you'll soon learn. Nat didn't know any more, with much less excuse."

"He was about as much use as a dying duck in a thunderstorm. Still, I was thankful he had told me about our obligation to inform our shareholders of the offer; I did at least know that."

"Come to bed, love. You'll feel better after a good night's rest."

"If it had been Jonathan, I'd have broken his damned neck."

"But it wasn't."

"I wished I'd had Jonathan with me, really. He knows how to talk their language. But Susie! I shall never feel the same to her again, never."

"I hope you weren't cross with her down the 'phone," said Ruth uneasily.

"I don't remember," said Chuff with truth.

At two o'clock next morning the bedside telephone rang. Ruth answered it.

"It's Jonathan, Chuff."

Jonathan's voice was wild and uneven.

"Chuff? You'd better come, Chuff."

"Come?" said Chuff, half asleep.

"Susie fell into premature labour after your telephone call. Everything went wrong. She was in the house alone. There was fog and I was late home and we didn't get to the hospital quickly. She has given birth, but she's very ill. They think she's sinking. She may not last till morning. You'd better come."

"I'll be with you in an hour," said Chuff, springing out of bed.

"Shall I come with you, Chuff?" said Ruth.

"No. No. For God's sake, no. Oh lord. Susie."

He dressed.

"The fog's gone. It's clear," said Ruth, drawing back a curtain.

"Good. I can make good time."

"Do drive carefully, Chuff."

"I always do."

This was true. He was a sensible if selfish driver. Though he was unfamiliar with the route, on the quiet night roads, the only sound the water dripping from the trees, he made good speed and reached his destination well under the time he had allowed himself. His concentration on reaching the hospital rapidly and his pleasure in doing so had driven the reason for his haste out of his mind, and this blankness lasted till he had climbed the steps to the great building. But here at the top he was met by Jonathan, pale, ravaged, his eyes burning, and Chuff's assurance fell from him. His tongue suddenly felt numb and swollen, unable to utter.

"How is she?" he managed to get out.

"They say she's just holding her own. Why did you shout at her down the telephone, Chuff?" said Jonathan. His eyes flashed, his tone was dangerous.

"Because by selling her Morcar shares she's destroyed Henry Morcar Limited, that's why," said Chuff, never backward in defence of himself.

"A life is worth more than a few shares."

"Henry Morcar Limited is my life."

"You care more for that than for Susie."

"No, I don't," said Chuff irritably, colouring. "But I care. Did you know anything of this share-selling, Jonathan? Eh?"

"No."

"I'm glad to hear that. I'd have broken your neck if you had."

"Try," said Jonathan, savagely as before.

"Well, I think you ought to have known."

"I agree," said Jonathan more mildly. "But she's been so much better lately that I thought——"

"Well, obviously she isn't. She can't—you'll have to keep a sharper watch on her in the future, Jonathan."

"If she has a future," said Jonathan turning away.

"Is it as bad as that?" said Chuff sorrowfully.

Jonathan nodded. They stood for a moment in silence, united by their grief. Then Chuff stirred.

"Well, can't we see her or something?" he said, moving restlessly towards the reception desk. "I'm sure it would do her good to see me, Jonathan."

"I can't say I'm sure of that."

"Let's try anyway."

He explained his relationship to Susie to the night porter, Jonathan gave the name of the ward, the porter telephoned, and presently the two men found themselves traversing end-less broad corridors. The smell of anaesthetic, the occasional glimpse of shadowed wards with humped beds where patients lay in pain, the encounters with nurses carrying basins of who-knew-what horrors, drained Chuff's courage; he could hardly force his limbs to move. Jonathan seemed more composed; of course he had done this ghastly journey before. But his pallor was alarming.

They were met at the door of the ward by the Night Sister, who surveyed them dourly.

"I told you to go home," she said to Jonathan, who made no reply.

"Mrs Oldroyd is having a very disturbed night," she continued. "We are just going to put her under heavier sedation."

"Let me see her first," urged Chuff.

"Very well. But I don't know how she'll stand it. If I say *out* it means out at once," said Sister.

She led them into the ward and drew a curtain. Chuff

found himself looking down at his sister's lovely face, now as of white marble, with the corners of the mouth turned down so as to wreck her beauty. Jonathan sat beside her, and taking her hand in his raised it to his lips. Susie's eyes slightly opened, she slightly smiled.

"Susie," said Chuff.

"Chuff!" cried Susie, opening her eyes in a terrible look of fear. Her marble cheek coloured feverishly. She shrank back against her pillows, clutched Jonathan's hand. "No! No!"

"Out!" said the Sister with emphasis, seizing Chuff's shoulder.

If one was a Morcar and an Oldroyd, reflected Chuff grimly, one took no notice of orders of that sort.

"I'm sorry I was so cross on the telephone, love," he said. "I didn't mean it, you know."

"You said I ruined you."

"Oh, pooh! You don't want to take any notice of that," said Chuff comfortably. "I was just letting off a bit of steam."

"Isn't it true, then?"

"Of course, not."

"Truthfully, Chuff?"

"Truthfully," said Chuff, choking a little.

The colour in Susie's cheeks sank to a more natural hue and she sighed, Chuff thought with relief. He bent forward and gently kissed her. "And now out you go," said Sister, digging her fingers viciously into Chuff's arm. "You'd better go too, Mr Oldroyd. I'll call you if there's any change."

Chuff yielded, allowing himself to be hustled out beyond the curtains; Jonathan quietly followed. The two men left the ward, and began the long trek back to the entrance.

"What about the—child?" demanded Chuff. He wanted to know if it had been born alive or dead, but had not the nerve to make such a crude enquiry.

"They are both living, but very frail, I understand."

"They?"

"Twins."

"Twins?" gasped Chuff.

"Girl twins."

Two female Oldroyds! In spite of himself Chuff could not help smiling a little. Why twins should always appear laugh-worthy to a man he did not know, but so it was. He suppressed his smile firmly. Poor Susie!

"I hope they'll all do well," he said uneasily. "Susie, I mean, and the girls."

"So do I," said Jonathan.

His tone was grim. They reached the hospital entrance. Chuff took down his coat from the hook where he had left it, and put it on. Jonathan watched him without making the slightest movement to assist.

"I hope you're satisfied with what you've done today, Chuff," he said.

"I'm sorry," said Chuff, trying unsuccessfully—his fingers seemed numb—to button his coat. It was an expensive garment, short, well-cut, of heavy wool-cum-man-made-fibre, Morcar cloth, and Chuff felt that Jonathan guessed its origin and regarded it as an added insult.

"I'm sorry," he repeated.

Jonathan with an impatient exclamation turned on his heel and walked sharply away into the waiting room.

Chuff drove home badly. He actually lost his way, found himself on one of those appallingly steep lanes which spring up from West Riding valleys, and only by the most deter-mined obstinacy, the firmest self-control, at last got himself back on to a main road, ten miles from where he had intended. It was almost dawn when he reached Stanney Royd. Ruth after one look at his face asked him nothing, but helped him silently off with his clothes and into bed. He was so exhausted that in spite of his mental torment he fell heavily asleep.

When he awoke there was daylight; he turned his wrist and saw that the time was after eleven o'clock. Usually when he awoke he felt cheerful; what was this frightful worry which spoiled everything this morning? He remembered—Susie. Ruth was approaching him with a cup of coffee and the morning newspaper. He looked at her, trying to judge her expression, not venturing to put the question for the answer he longed to hear.

"Jonathan telephoned," said Ruth gravely. "Susie shows a slight improvement this morning."

Chuff gave a long heavy sigh of relief. And immediately, that anxiety being relieved, his other trouble poured over him and weighed him to the ground. What was going to become of Henry Morcar Limited? He opened the *Yorkshire Post*; in the business section a column was headed by a paragraph announcing the proposed merger.

Chuff sprang from bed and made haste to Syke Mill.

4

NEGOTIATIONS

HALF A SCORE men, of various ages and from various departments, were standing glowering in his office. Miss Sprott fluttered about looking terrified and Chuff told her to summon the heads of departments in half an hour's time. Acting a calmness he did not feel, he took off his coat and hat and hung it up, then seating himself at his desk enquired quietly:

"Something wrong?"

"We've come about this takeover," said one of the older men.

"It's a merger, not a takeover," said Chuff irritably.

"Looks the same to us. What will it mean exactly, like?"

"I hope it won't mean anything. I don't want a merger or a takeover, any more than you do."

"Well, you see, Syke Mill's our lives. We been here a long time, some of us. We been all right here, with your grandfather."

"I'm not my grandfather."

"Us can see that," said a young voice sardonically.

"And these times are not his times. Everything is different, and these mergers are all the fashion."

"Well, we don't want no merger."

"Neither do I," said Chuff savagely.

"Shall you turn it down, then?"

"If I can."

There was a murmur of dissatisfaction and the men shuffled their feet uneasily.

"You needn't worry!" shouted Chuff suddenly, losing his

temper: "The larger the firm is, the more you'll prosper."

The quick elation on the young men's faces, the slow brightening of some of the elders', sickened him.

"Well, if that's all," he began, taking up a letter at random from his desk.

But here there was an interruption; the Syke Mill shop steward, a dark, capable, fiery young man in his thirties, burst furiously into the room.

"I don't know what you think you're about!" he shouted at the men. "It's my job to undertake all negotiations with the management, remember!"

"We come about this takeover—or merger, or whatever you call it," said the spokesman. "We've heard as how sometimes mills are closed down in these mergers, and we want to know what's going on."

He spoke in an obstinate manner and was evidently determined to have his say; the men behind him murmured: "That's right," and the shop steward changed his tune.

"Aye, and no wonder!" he exclaimed. "We've been shabbily tret. You leave us to read about it in the newspaper, Mr Chuff. It's not right, that isn't. Old Mr Morcar would never have done that to us. You should have told us before."

"I didn't know about it myself till yesterday afternoon," said Chuff, exaggerating a little to improve his case.

"Well then, you should have been here first thing this morning to tell us."

"I agree with you," said Chuff. "But my sister was dangerously ill in childbirth and I had to drive to Lorimer at two o'clock in the morning."

"Well, of course we hope she's better," said the shop steward crossly.

"There's a slight improvement this morning and the twins are said to be doing well," said Chuff, despising himself for using his private affairs to soften their hostility.

The younger men frowned and moved uneasily, disliking this reference to the results of their pleasures, but the older men's faces softened.

"But how can they take Syke over?" objected the previous spokesman. "They can't just walk in and say it's theirs."

"They will buy up the shares from the shareholders," began Chuff.

"Shareholders! Isn't that capitalism all over?" cried the shop steward. "Just because they've got a bit of money a few chaps can walk in and take our lives from us."

"That's right—true enough—we don't count," said the men.

"Not if I can help it," said Chuff.

There was a pause. The sounds of the department heads gathering outside could now be heard.

"Well—we just come to tell you how we feel," said the spokesman.

"I take it you will keep us informed of the progress of the negotiations," said the shop steward.

"I will. I promise you, I give you my word that I shall do my utmost to fight off this threat," said Chuff.

The men made a move towards the door.

"You might ask me if there were anything you could do to help me fight it off," Chuff reproached them.

They halted.

"Well, is there?"

"We need a very good year."

The younger men jeered. "Aw, increased productivity! We're tired of hearing that."

"*Sick* and tired."

"It'd help you, but not us."

The shop steward hesitated.

"How would it help against a merger?" he asked.

"If the shareholders' shares earn them good money here,

they won't want to sell. That might put the price of their shares up to beyond what these merger people, Messrs Hamsun, would want to pay," said Chuff, feeling grateful to Messrs Alfriston and Howard for this information.

"Capitalism!" sneered the shop steward again.

"Well, think it over," said Chuff.

They made no reply, but Chuff guessed that from then onwards the mill would hum with talk.

"What does Major Armitage think about it all, then?" said the shop steward in Chuff's ear, as the men took themselves out.

"He believes in the productivity idea as much as I do," said Chuff.

"We haven't had a major clash in the textile trade for nigh on forty years," said the shop steward in a conciliatory tone.

Chuff felt a passionate longing to exclaim: "That's not your fault, I'm sure!" But he controlled himself, and said mildly:

"It's a good record."

The heads of departments came in, and Chuff announced the threatened merger to them with suitable gravity. They understood the points he made, only too well.

For the next five months Chuff's life seemed entirely occupied by Messrs Hamsun's proposition. He went often to London, and was soon wearied to death of Alfriston and Howard's fine premises; he hated the breakfast train and loathed even more the late night return. The press pestered him. Mr Alfriston dealt ably with reporters, but press announcements brought telephone calls to Chuff from everybody in the West Riding, as it seemed to him. The whole textile trade hummed with gossip, and when Chuff made an entrance anywhere men's faces lighted with interest, and they bore down on him, avid for news, like hyenas for flesh, Chuff thought. Frequent meetings were held with the Hamsuns, uncle and nephew, and the advisers on both sides. The senior Hamsun, John, in his fifties, a handsome rather impatient man, was the picture of a top business executive, but came out with some remarks which revealed his very considerable knowledge of textile markets, while the nephew (whose name, for heaven's sake, was Cyril), lean, bald and ugly, seemed to know everything about Trade Union rates, welfare services, S.E.T., company tax, Pension Schemes, redundancy, in fact, everything about modern business management which Chuff did not know. Everything was conducted in courteous terms, for Mr Alfriston had murmured privately to Chuff: "Mud always sticks to the thrower," and Chuff commanded himself to believe this axiom and act accordingly. To conceal, to some extent, the crimson tide which rushed to his face when he was upset, he developed a habit of stroking his left eyebrow with two fingers in a thoughtful way, while he pushed his temper below boiling point.

"We had thought, Mr Morcar, that our firms could be of mutual assistance in capturing the European market," said Mr John Hamsun.

"I don't feel in need of assistance," replied Chuff cheerfully.

"You are very young, Mr Morcar," said John Hamsun after a pause.

"I don't consider my five years' textile course at Annotsfield Technical College—though it's the best in the country—counts for much," said Chuff in his politest tones, "but my years under my grandfather's tuition are a different matter."

"But that is just what we are saying, Mr Morcar. Our skills are complementary."

Not being absolutely sure what *complementary* meant in this connection, Chuff smiled blandly and was silent.

Of course there were occasions when this surface courtesy cracked a little and the reality grinned through. There was the meeting, for example, when Cyril Hamsun observed bluntly: "The day of the family business is over." After this, Nat Armitage somehow dropped out; he could never make it convenient to come to the discussions, and Chuff felt more free without him. At the next meeting Chuff broke out: "You care only for profit, not for product or personnel." He thought this rather clever, and repeated it. The Hamsuns were angered and brought out rapidly quantities of facts and statistics to prove the high quality of their cloths and their paternal care for their workpeople.

After this there was silence for some weeks; Chuff at first lived on a rack of suspense, but was beginning happily to hope that the attack had been withdrawn when suddenly Cyril Hamsun rang him up, and after polite enquiries about Ruth—the Hamsuns learned somehow, probably through Nat and Alfriston and Howard, of the approaching birth— said cheerfully:

"Sorry, old chap, we know how you feel but we mean to go on."

Chuff, his hopes thus all dashed, felt positively sick as he laid the telephone down. Almost immediately the bell rang again, and Mrs Jessopp announced excitedly that Mrs Morcar had gone to the hospital, and birth could probably be expected before nightfall.

Ruth had a normal, reasonably swift delivery, and the child proved to be a fair-complexioned, lively, bouncy, robust boy, with a pugnacious little face, much like his father's, and a hearty cry; no anxiety was ever felt about *him*. Perhaps it was this, but more likely his Hamsun worries, which caused Chuff to feel comparatively indifferent to a birth which he had previously anticipated with eager tenderness. Mrs. Mellor came to stay at Stanney Royd for a few weeks, to give

Ruth a helping hand, but this was from wish rather than necessity, for Ruth went about radiant with happiness, well able to cope with the child's requirements and rejoicing in fulfilling them. The parents had long ago made up their minds that, if they had a son, they would call him simply *Henry*. Ruth still assumed that this choice held, and though the threat to its special relevance made Chuff wince, he allowed it to stand. Jonathan and G.B. became his godfathers, Susie his godmother, Jonathan sending a silver mug engraved H.M. with a card attached to its handle, saying: *To Hal, with love from his aunt and uncle*. Ruth took a fancy to the nickname of Hal, and Chuff let that pass too, though he thought it an impertinence on Jonathan's part. Chuff invited Nathan to the christening, but Nathan was not well enough to come—rheumatism, the curse of the West Riding.

"My son's being christened today," said Chuff to the shop steward, as he encountered him in the warehouse. "I should like to give you all a holiday—but I shan't. Productivity, you know."

"Are we winning, Mr Chuff?" said the young man.

His tone was sympathetic, and the association of himself with the mill also surprised Chuff. There seemed a silence in the room, and looking about he perceived that all the men present were gazing at him.

"About the merger, you mean? I don't know, Jack. They're tough and they're determined and they've got a lot of money. I'm doing my best."

"Good luck, then," said Jack, and turned away abruptly, ashamed of this display of sentiment.

That the Syke Mill labour force (as the Hamsuns would call the men, reflected Chuff sardonically) seemed all to have come round to his side and be backing him energetically— this was certainly true; productivity was up and there were fewer errors—surprised Chuff the more because recently he

had behaved disagreeably to the men. He toured the departments indefatigably, and always in a bad temper; scowling,
questioning sharply, bawling them out. This was especially
the case with the Design Department; he entered like a
whirlwind, demanding fiercely when they were going to give
him some patterns fit to show to Messrs Hamsun, something
new.

"They'll be on the pattern looms next week," said Mr
Simmonds.

"Can't you get a move on?"

He observed that whereas Mr Simmonds, though his dried
elderly face flushed, and he reared his head in a bridling
action, replied stiffly, "We are doing our best, Mr Chuff,"
Paul Yarrow winced and shrank.

"He's afraid," thought Chuff brutally. "He's the sort to
make mistakes when he's afraid. I'd better calm down."

He spoke in a smooth silky tone to Yarrow but noticed
that the young man's hands still shook.

He returned to his office to find Alfriston and Howard on
the telephone summoning him to a meeting with the Hamsuns and their advisers on the morrow.

"What is it this time?"

"They have prepared their letter to go out to your shareholders," said Mr Alfriston. "They think it right to show it to
you and receive your comments personally, before sending
it to press."

That was the worst of those damned Hamsuns, thought
Chuff irritably; they were always so damned correct.

"After you have seen it your Board can take its final
decision and draft its own letter—recommending acceptance
or rejection, as the case may be."

"This is the crunch," thought Chuff, and he replied cheerfully, "I have all my figures ready, but I prefer to see their
letter before drafting mine."

The Hamsun letter was impressive. On thick white paper, in very legible print, it stated succinctly all the advantages, to both sides, of a merger. The central paragraph, in lettering remarkably black, offered 45s. for a Morcar share, or 17s. 6d. and one Hamsun group share. To anyone who knew the prospering affairs of the Hamsun group—and they had been well publicised in the press of late—this latter offer was very tempting, thought Chuff.

"The lay-out is striking," commented Alfriston, and tapping the central paragraph he referred to the fount of type by name.

"What do you say to this, Mr Morcar?" demanded Howard.

"It is our final offer," said Cyril Hamsun. "And remember, Mr Morcar, if we don't take you over, somebody else will. You won't get a better offer than ours."

"I should like three days to consider," said Chuff.

"You're a very obstinate young man, Mr Morcar," said the elder Hamsun irritably.

"That is so," agreed Chuff with a wide smile.

"Well, take your three days," said John Haumsn, shrugging.

The meeting thereupon broke up, and Chuff caught the earlier train.

5

DIVERSION

WHEN HE REACHED Annotsfield the night was dark, cold, and as usual, rainy. He felt weary and irritable almost beyond bearing as he recalled for a moment the African sun of his boyhood. The thought of driving through this poor visibility up the Ire Valley filled him with sick disgust. As he crossed the station square to his car he trod, as it chanced, the very spot where Henry Morcar had lost his life. It was the last straw. If he had been a woman, reflected Chuff, he would have burst into tears; as it was he gave a fierce exclamation, and swinging aside rapidly, charged into the Lion Hotel which filled almost the whole of one side of the square.

This hostelry, the resort of textile men since the early nineteenth century, massively rebuilt in the prosperous '70's, allowed to grow shabby in the dreadful '30's, had recently refurbished itself in the modern style, so that the bar was equipped with lots of strip lighting, white paint and tall plaid-seated stools. It was crammed with men accompanied here and there by handsomely dressed women, the air was thick with smoke, everyone was talking at the top of their voices. Chuff bought himself a stiff whisky and looked around. He raised a hand in greeting to two or three men he knew, but hardly felt on sufficiently intimate terms to join them. It occurred to him that he was lonely. In an alcove by the huge old chimney breast—now of course occupied by an electric fire—he glimpsed a face he knew. It was Paul Yarrow's; the brown eyes gazed at him yearningly. Chuff crossed the room. Weaving his way through the knotted groups was tiresome, but on the other hand it was agreeable to look purposeful.

"Good evening, Paul," he said.

"Good evening, Mr Morcar," replied Yarrow.

Chuff was faintly surprised, for in the mill he was usually addressed as *Mr Chuff*. But immediately he understood; Yarrow was accompanied by a woman, and did not wish to use a form which implied subordination.

"My wife," said Yarrow.

"Oh, good evening, Mrs Yarrow," said Chuff, surprised to find that Yarrow was married.

He then remembered, however, that the Technical College Principal had mentioned a Yarrow wife, describing her as an artist. What a piece, he thought, whew! Her mini-skirt was so extremely short that as she perched on a stool which had been pushed aside from the bar, her crotch was almost visible. But her legs are worth it, thought Chuff, admiring their slenderness and length. She saw his look and swung one foot to retain his attention. Her pale red hair, lacquered to a high gloss, was piled up on her head in elaborate convolutions; her features were regular and handsome; her light grey eyes were heavily made up with green eye-shadow and mascara; her very long golden-red eyelashes (if you could call them *hers*, thought Chuff sardonically) curled over an ivory cheek. Her breasts were disappointingly small, quite overshadowed by the thick strings of rose, green and mauve beads which hung between them, but her arms, bare to the shoulder, were perfect, white and rounded, and decorated with golden bracelets which clinked as she gave him her hand. Rather clumsy hands, but with long pointed nails painted mauve to match her skin-tight dress. Yes, quite a piece, thought Chuff; how on earth did poor Yarrow manage to pick her up?

They talked. About the weather—Mrs Yarrow thought the West Riding weather was simply the worst in the world. About his frequent journeys to London, for which she envied

him—and if she lived in London, New York would be the
only desirable place to her, thought Chuff. Her voice was a
high but not unpleasing drawl, with no trace of accent.

"You're not a West Riding native, then, Mrs Yarrow?"
he said.

"Heavens, no! I'm from the south. You can take the West
Riding and drop it in the North Sea, for all I care. Or
perhaps the Atlantic would be better."

"Deeper," suggested Chuff.

"That's right."

She laughed and blinked her eyes at him.

"Can't we have another drink, Paul?" she said then
pettishly.

"Of course," said her husband meekly, collecting her glass.

"Not for me, thanks," said Chuff.

"Oh do. Why not? Cheer up and have another," she said,
bending her head on one side and looking up at him coquet-
tishly as her husband, no doubt relieved, for whisky was
dear, accepted Chuff's refusal and went off to the bar.

"Please do, to please me."

"I have to drive myself home, Mrs Yarrow."

"Do call me Lois."

Chuff said nothing, but he had a pleasurable sensation.
To forget his merger preoccupation for a moment was an
immense relief; to lean against the mantelpiece in the Lion
bar, drinking whisky and talking to a woman who was
obviously flirting with him, made him feel agreeably man-
of-the-world.

Yarrow was having difficulty in getting attention at the
bar counter—he always would, reflected Chuff; he was of
that type.

"Don't you find the West Riding the last word in bore-
dom?" pursued Lois.

"Not particularly."

D

"Ah, you make your own amusements."

"When I get the chance."

"The afternoon is the loneliest time," said Lois softly.

She looked into his eyes for a long moment before dropping her gaze.

Chuff was not particularly conceited about his person, to which indeed apart from seeing that it was well groomed and well clad, he gave little attention. He thought he was a decent figure of a man and left it at that. But it was impossible not to perceive the invitation in Lois's words and tone. *She's taken a fancy to me*, he thought, and he felt flattered. *I'm a better man than Yarrow, anyway.* Accordingly when the drinks Yarrow fetched were finished, he offered to drive them home.

"We're only just round the corner," protested Yarrow, "in the new block of flats there."

"It's pouring with rain and Mrs Yarrow will get wet," said Chuff as Lois drew a very inadequate fur stole round her shoulders.

"It's very kind of you, Mr Morcar," simpered Lois.

Chuff went out and brought his car to the hotel door, took the Yarrows aboard and delivered them dry to their towering block. "Flats are convenient," he reflected. "You might be visiting anyone."

Lois made no secret of the fact that the handsome car impressed her. Chuff, who loved his car, was naturally pleased.

"Won't you come in for a last drink?" she urged, as Chuff held the door for her and she descended, showing, of course, a really eye-catching length of silken leg.

"No, thanks," said Chuff, and added in a low tone: "Not now."

They exchanged glances, and the rendezvous being thus settled, Chuff excused himself by saying aloud that the hour was late and he had had a heavy day.

He slept well, and awoke refreshed and full of fighting spirit. Sitting up in bed, though it was still early, he rang Jonathan.

"How is Susie?"

"She is at home now," replied Jonathan carefully.

The reserve in his tone took Chuff aback.

"But surely—isn't she all right by now?" he said.

"She is improving steadily," said Jonathan, as before.

Chuff gave it up and proceeded to his real business.

"Is there a good printer in this district?" he said. "Somebody who prints letterheads and things? A really artistic printer? Do you know a really artistic printer in the West Riding?"

"But of course," said Jonathan, naming one. "Their work's known all over England."

"Thanks," said Chuff. "Give my love to Susie."

He rang off. Getting to Syke Mill in good time, he coped rapidly with the routine jobs which awaited him, then settled to the composition of his recommendation to the shareholders to reject the Hamsun's offer. It was indeed *his* recommendation, for he had had to bully the other members of the Henry Morcar Board to agree. He had read to them a rather woolly draft, which they had to some extent amended; but now that he had the Hamsuns' letter in front of him as a guide, he made a much better job of it. He was talking to Jonathan's printer by lunch-time.

"This is of the utmost importance and I must have a dozen copies by tomorrow evening."

"That is an unreasonable demand and its fulfilment could be costly."

"I don't care about the cost. I have to take them to London the following day by the early train."

"Very well. Could you call for them? By the way, I think there is a slip here," said the distinguished-looking master

printer, pointing an exquisitely sharpened pencil at a word
in the last line.

"How did that get in?" exclaimed Chuff, allowing the
printer to make the necessary grammatical alteration, as he
himself could not have done so. "Look. This is the important
piece. I want this forecast of next year's profits to stand out,
to catch the eye."

"Bolder type?" suggested the printer.

"Their letter has that. The people opposing us, you know.
I don't want to copy," said Chuff virtuously.

"We could inset."

"Do that," said Chuff recklessly, hoping he was right.

"Inset *and* bolder type, I think."

"I leave it to you with perfect confidence," said Chuff,
hoping this flattery sounded sincere.

He took a late lunch in the printer's city, drove back to
Annotsfield, parked his car in the station square amid
hundreds of others, and walked round the corner to the
Yarrows' block of flats. The time was just right; it was the
middle of the afternoon, when every employed person was
safely enclosed in his place of work.

Lois opened the door to him.

"Mr Morcar!" she said in a tone of surprise, quite
artificial and intended to be recognised as such. There was
no doubt she was pleased. Her pale eyes gleamed and she
smiled.

The sound of his grandfather's name gave Chuff a mo-
mentary qualm, but he suppressed it. After all, Henry
Morcar himself was not sexually blameless.

Lois was dressed today in black tights, with a violently
patterned tunic in green and black, skin-tight and very short.
It looked expensive, and Chuff wondered whether she had
private resources to supplement her husband's salary. But
no; she would not have married such a timid little twerp in

that case. Thick green wooden beads hung round her neck.
"Do come in."

She led him into a largish well-lighted room, sparsely
furnished with attractive but (to Chuff) strangely shaped
chairs. Around the walls were hung several abstract paintings.
Chuff knew nothing about art but at once judged them to be
bad, because he wished to despise Lois. One or two, very
bright, which caught his fancy, he immediately assumed to
be her husband's.

"Do sit down," she said, and as he hesitated, pushed him
into a corner of the settee—a large wide piece of furniture,
well cushioned, designed precisely for Chuff's purpose. Her
push, though meant to be playful, was strong, muscular; she
was no timid gentle girl. Chuff's scruples, if he had ever had
any, vanished.

"A cup of tea?" suggested Lois, smiling maliciously—she
knew too well what he had come for.

"Nonsense," said Chuff.

She switched on a record. The heavy monotonous beat of
pop music, shouted rather than sung, in a raucous tuneless
untrained voice, inflamed Chuff's senses. They did not need
it; his impatience grew as Lois began to dance, twisting her
body in elaborate convolutions which displayed its every line
to advantage. She was older than she probably wished to be
thought, decided Chuff, but not bad all the same; her breasts
were small but firm, her long legs, a little too plump in the
upper parts, were otherwise agreeably slender. Her green
beads swung from side to side; with an impatient gesture she
threw them off. They landed on the settee; Chuff with equal
carelessness pitched them to a nearby chair. Lois laughed
approvingly, and her pale eyes gleamed.

She held out her hand to him, inviting him to join her in
the dance. Chuff shook his head, but seizing her wrist as she
passed, pulled her down to the settee beside him and took

her strongly in his arms. She gave a pleased little laugh and, nestling in a competent manner against his shoulder, laid a hand between his thighs.

"Oh, my!" she exclaimed, rolling her eyes.

Chuff took her roughly. She was ready and eager. The green shift offered no difficulties; the absence of beads was a relief; the tights were tiresome, but she helped him with them. She was better in bed than Ruth, he realised; altogether, it was a satisfying experience, though, he freely admitted, a dirty one.

MERGER

IT WAS OBVIOUS that Chuff's beautifully printed letter of rejection made a favourable impression on the Hamsuns. Or rather, an *un*favourable impression, thought Chuff, for of course, the better it was, the more it might influence its recipients to decline the sale of their shares. The Hamsuns clearly thought it persuasive.

"You know we would much rather have you with us, recommending acceptance to your shareholders, Mr Morcar," said the elder Hamsun.

"How can I possibly recommend acceptance when I don't know what you plan to do with the firm when you've got it? If you plan to make your headquarters elsewhere and close Syke Mill, you can whistle for it."

"We don't propose to close Syke Mill, good heavens!" began Cyril.

"Of course, the new road may come," put in Chuff, honest in spite of himself.

"Our information is that the plans are likely to be changed, and only a small corner will be lopped off," said Alfriston smoothly.

"How do you learn these things?" exclaimed Chuff, astounded.

"We have our sources."

"The Syke Mill premises are still good, and the equipment thoroughly up to date. Daisy Mill we could close; another of our subsidiaries—we have five—does the same work under better conditions."

"And what about the Daisy men?" demanded Chuff, imagining what Jonathan would say to this.

"We should take them in at Syke, for which we envisage expansion."

"But that's just what you couldn't," cried Chuff. "It's miles from where they live."

"Only two miles, I think."

"But it's in another valley. You can't go over the top, you've got to go round the bases of the hills. You don't know the West Riding."

They looked at him thoughtfully.

"A company bus, perhaps?" murmured Cyril.

"And Old Mill?" said Chuff.

"The fabric is hopelessly antiquated."

"But the site by the river is of course very valuable," put in Alfriston.

"My Oldroyd ancestors worked there in 1812," said Chuff.

"Our business is a prospering textile trade, not sentiment," said Cyril.

"And ours is sound finance," said Alfriston firmly.

"Surely it's better for the Old Mill to contribute to the country's prosperity, rather than moulder into a museum," urged the senior Hamsun.

"There are only two ways for you to succeed in the modern textile world, Mr Morcar," said Alfriston. "One: you can stay independent and small, and run short lengths off your looms, of some very high-class special cloth, for which you charge very high prices. Or: you can merge, and become part of an enormous group running long lengths for popular consumption all over the world."

"That is absolutely correct," approved the elder Hamsun. "You have described the contemporary situation exactly, Mr Alfriston."

"Charles, join us," said Cyril.

Charles, indeed! thought Chuff sardonically. "I might if I could have my own terms," he threw out.

"And what are they?"

"A five years' contract as managing director of Syke Mill, with option of renewal; redundancy payments for all the Daisy men——"

"Redundancy payments are a legal requirement everywhere," murmured Cyril.

"—retention of the name of Henry Morcar Limited—you can put *Subsidiary of the Hamsun Group* below that, if you like; retention of high quality in the product; a considerable block of shares in the Group in part exchange for some of my Morcar holdings. And a seat on the Group Board, of course. I think that's about all," said Chuff, laughing harshly.

The two Hamsuns looked at each other.

"Well, I think I could get our Board to agree to that," said the elder Hamsun at length.

"Better get it agreed and down in writing before we issue the letter of approach to shareholders," said Alfriston, seizing the dumbfounded Chuff's arm and hustling him to his feet. "We'll each jot down the terms and compare, shall we?"

"But surely," said Chuff when they were alone together in Alfriston's private office, "they don't mean to agree to all that, do they?"

"Why not? They have come to appreciate your merits in the course of the negotiations, Mr Morcar. If I may say so, you have yourself perhaps acquired useful experience, have you not. The prospect before the group is a splendid one. Of course, the Morcar letter to shareholders must be rewritten."

When Chuff left the firm of Alfriston and Howard, he turned aside from the lift and walked down the marble stairway. Out of sight of the landing, he sat down on the cold steps and buried his head in his hands. He did not know whether he had behaved like a coward or a hero. On the whole he thought: both.

IV

THE NEW GENERATION

1

TWO SONS

IN THE NEXT few months Chuff worked harder than he had ever done before.

All the Henry Morcar shareholders joyously accepted the Hamsun 45s. offer—as well they might—and congratulated Chuff on the firm stand which had secured this fine price for them. All that is, except Nathan, who wept and went back to bed with another alleged attack of rheumatism.

"He feels he's nothing left to live for, you see, Mr Chuff," said Nathan's wife when Chuff called to see the old works manager. (Her over-permed grey hair and long skirt marked her as belonging to a passing generation.) "With losing our Jack in the War, and then Mr Morcar and now Syke Mill you see, he's lost heart like."

At this Chuff rushed up the stairs to the neat little bedroom where Nathan lay quietly against his pillow, sad and resigned.

"Now look here, Nathan," he burst forth, "if you think you're going to die and leave me holding the baby, you can think again. You can't die for ten years yet."

Nathan, astounded by this address, said feebly, "Why?"

"Because I need you. I've got to do the job so well that I remain managing director of Henry Morcar Limited when my contract finishes in five years, and I can't do it without you.'

"It's very good of you to say so," murmured Nathan.

"Nonsense. It's pure selfishness."

Nathan, though hobbling about on a stick, returned to work on the following Monday morning.

Of course Chuff had an outrageous scene with the Daisy

Mill men. When he announced the merger to them they shouted at him in a great deep-throated roar, and even shook their fists.

"What's to become of us?"

"Redundancy pay——"

"To hell with redundancy pay."

But Chuff had considerable physical courage and did not doubt it; he shouted back at them and on the whole enjoyed the row. In truth he sympathised with their grievance, but was not going to sell his side by admitting it. Hamsun's kept urging him to give all at Daisy provisional notice, but he postponed this, enquiring where Syke Mill was to get its cloths finished if Daisy fell out of existence before their subsidiary was ready to take the load; and this waiting for something to turn up was rewarded, for suddenly a great flood of orders fell upon Syke, and through Syke upon Daisy. Everybody was madly busy and rushed about whistling cheerfully.

This agreeable development was largely due to one of Paul Yarrow's designs, which even Mr Simmonds enthusiastically announced to be almost as good as one of old Mr Morcar's. Yarrow smiled at this unhappy comparison when congratulated; he looked so miserable nowadays that Chuff sometimes wondered whether his afternoon visits to Lois had been discovered. But on the whole, he thought not; he had imposed the severest discretion.

"No letters, no 'phone calls," he had said.

Lois pouted. "And how are you going to make me conform to your rules?"

"If you don't, it's all over," said Chuff cheerfully.

"You're so kind and considerate," sneered Lois, flushing. "I suppose it's no use asking you to pay a bill or two for me."

"None. But I don't mind contributing," said Chuff, drawing out his wallet and beginning to extract a few five-pound notes.

Like many people with red hair, Lois had a quick temper. It flamed now.

"Mr C. H. F. Morcar, I like you less every time I see you!" she shouted.

"I feel just the same way about you," retorted Chuff cheerfully.

"I wonder you trouble to come here at all," cried Lois, furious.

"There's a reason for that," said Chuff.

He laughed, and after a moment Lois laughed too. They made love—not that either of them ever thought of it as love —as usual; Lois accepted four of the five-pound notes, and Chuff continued to visit her in the afternoons.

With his present business preoccupations, he had really hardly time for sexual dalliance—"a merger and a mistress on the same programme," he told himself sardonically, "is a bit much"—but he enjoyed putting half an hour with Lois into a day already crammed with engagements.

For there were legal and financial arrangements to make, which seemed to go on for ever; countless letters to dictate— Miss Sprott proved really very good, but had to have a junior to help. Chuff had to visit all the other five subsidiary companies, and their boards of directors all had to visit him; Chuff paid increasing tribute to his grandfather as he discovered how little he could learn from them, how much they could learn from Syke Mill. There were Group Boards to attend, at first very nerve-racking but Chuff grew used to them. Cyril Hamsun telephoned him at ten o'clock every morning. At first he felt this as an evidence of subordination which chafed him, but presently he grew to appreciate it as an evidence of Cyril's favour. They had become friendly, using first names to each other, and though they never quite gossiped about the other Hamsun directors' failings, came enjoyably near it. Chuff learned to play golf, to order meals in expensive restaurants, to cultivate that tone of disbelief about everything, which became a prosperous young executive.

He urged Ruth to spend more money on her clothes.

"I shan't," said Ruth flatly.

He noticed, however, that as the months passed by she did not keep to this decision; without mentioning the matter to him she began to frequent better shops than before and her taste became quieter.

One bright spring morning as Chuff was walking down the main street in Annotsfield—he had just bought a very expensive lorry and, having ordered it to be inscribed Henry Morcar Limited, was feeling pleased with himself—when he saw Ruth on the opposite side of the street. She was bare-headed, in a good dark suit of Morcar cloth; at her side, neat in grey wool, toddled Hal. They stopped beside a spotted rocking horse, which stood invitingly, no doubt for some charitable purpose, outside a toy-shop. Hal was not a very expressive child, but the agitation of his gestures now revealed very clearly, even across the street, a passionate desire to mount the horse. Ruth yielded and lifted the child into position on its back. The horse, however, being mounted on springs, now rocked, as became its name, and Hal evidently found this dizzy motion terrifying, for he let out a loud yell and clutched its mane. The yell was so loud that the whole street paused to look whence it came; here and there people even came out of shops in alarm. Chuff laughed, and dodging the traffic, crossed the street. Ruth looked flushed and embarrassed;. Hal, still loudly weeping, seemed divided in his wishes, for he hit at the horse with one hand and with the other, hit at his mother who was trying to take him away.

"Hey, hey!" said Chuff reprovingly. "What are you doing, you bad boy? You mustn't hit Mummy, that's naughty."

He gave Henry Morcar Junior a slight slap on the buttocks.

At once Hal's eyes and mouth opened to their widest extent; glancing at his father, he gave a look and a wail of such anguished stupefaction, as if the earth had crumbled beneath his feet, that Chuff was quite disconcerted.

"Well, come along then," he said in a consoling tone.

He picked the child up in his arms and set him on his shoulder. Hal's wail abruptly ceased; with a bland look of forgiving and forgetting, he put his arm in a casual accustomed style round his father's neck.

For Chuff it was a moment of deep and strangely contradictory emotion. On the one hand he felt—perhaps really for the first time—the pride of fatherhood. This little living human organism on his shoulder was *his* son; Chuff had created him. He would fight for Hal savagely; let no one attempt to harm this child. On the other hand he felt a terrible guilt; he had deprived the child of his birthright, for Henry Morcar Limited would not belong to Hal. He felt almost angry with Hal for being his victim, for throwing the responsibility for his existence and destiny upon his father. He wished with all his heart that he had chosen the other alternative which Alfriston suggested; a few fine cloths and independence. Look at Nat Armitage, making a little less profit every year, but unharassed by mergers and modern business methods. But would Hal have been satisfied by that? He looked up at the pugnacious little face, so like his own, and doubted it; Hal wanted to ride the horse though he was afraid of the animal. Just like his father, of course, Chuff admitted. But he felt in bondage to the next generation. "No sooner are you rid of the old generation than you're tied down by the new," he thought bitterly.

"He's often naughty," said Ruth.

"Boys will be boys," said Chuff mechanically.

"I wondered when you were going to take any real notice of him," said Ruth.

Her tone was a trifle acid, and Chuff would have been surprised if he had had time to think about it. But as usual, he had not.

That evening as the Morcars sat at their evening meal Mrs Jessopp ushered in Ruth's brother, G. B. Mellor.

"Why, G.B!" exclaimed Chuff cordially. He sprang up and invited the guest to join them. "Bring another plate, Mrs Jessopp."

"I've had my tea, thank you," said G.B., stiffly.

This was a mode of rebuke to the Morcars for abandoning the high tea customary with so many "ordinary" people in Yorkshire and taking to the loftier evening dinner. This had in any case been habitual at Stanney Royd before his grandfather's death, and Chuff felt vexed. "I shall eat when I like," he thought crossly. He observed, too, that G.B.'s expression was somewhat stern and disapproving, and his response to Ruth's sisterly embrace perfunctory.

"We haven't seen much of you since you went south," said Chuff in a cooler tone.

"I came to Annotsfield to tell my Mam of my good news," said G.B. as before. "So I thought I'd just drop in on you."

"What's the good news, then?" said Chuff, forcing an interested tone.

"I've been chosen as a future Parliamentary candidate," said G.B. more eagerly, naming the West Riding constituency concerned. "I was at their final meeting last night."

"Labour candidate, I presume," said Chuff sourly, while Ruth exclaimed with delight and enquired about the size of the Tory majority at the last election, and rejoiced to find it small.

"Of course I can't expect *you* to be pleased, Chuff, with your grand new merger and all."

"Your Government is always urging mergers as instruments of more efficiency and productivity," said Chuff, stiff in his turn.

At this point the telephone rang, and he went to the morning-room to answer it. The caller was Cyril Hamsun, as usual, and his subject a complicated matter of changing the specifications of a large order received recently from a multiple firm of tailors. The effort to remember accurately the original specification, the stage the cloths had reached, the possibility of alteration and new dates for delivery, was considerable, and when Chuff returned to the dining-room he felt irritably conscious that he appeared tired and harassed beside his brother-in-law, who looked particularly fresh and lively with his rosy cheeks, smooth thick dark hair, solid chunky body and expression of satisfaction.

"Well, I'll be off," said G.B., rising.

His tone was gruff, and Chuff did not try to detain him. Ruth took her brother to the front door, but Chuff made the excuse of his congealing food not to accompany them—he had had enough of G.B. for the present.

Next morning as he stood at the washstand in their bed-room shaving, Ruth said suddenly:

"Do you want a divorce, Chuff?"

"A what?" said Chuff without much interest, thinking he had misheard.

"A divorce."

"A divorce?" said Chuff, turning from the washstand in amazement. "What on earth are you talking about?"

"If you want a divorce so that you can marry that cheap little floozy, I will gladly bring the necessary proceedings," said Ruth in a loud clear tone.

"Don't use such language, Ruth," said Chuff, shocked. "It doesn't become you."

"It becomes me to speak it as much as it does you to do it," said Ruth.

The words were confused, but the meaning clear. Chuff was taken aback.

Suddenly becoming conscious that, razor in hand, lather on face, clad in an unromantic cotton vest, he was not looking his most attractive, he laid down the razor, wiped his face and put his shirt on hastily.

"I don't know what you mean, Ruth."

"Oh, yes, you do. Tell me, do you want a divorce?"

"Of course not. Don't be silly, Ruth."

"You love me, do you?"

"Of course, you're my wife."

There was a pause. They glared at each other.

"It was only a bit of fun," said Chuff at length, half apologetic, half furious.

"Fun!"

"Nowadays society is permissive."

"I'm being permissive," said Ruth hardly.

"How do you know about it, anyway?"

"All Annotsfield knows about it, I understand. If you think I enjoy being made to look a fool in front of the whole West Riding, you're mistaken."

"I should enjoy it if G.B. would mind his own business," growled Chuff, suddenly perceiving the origin of Ruth's knowledge.

"And how do you think I enjoy my brother telling me tales of my husband?"

"Well—I'm sorry."

"What's the use of that?" cried Ruth, exploding into loud tears.

Chuff went to her and tried rather half-heartedly to take her in his arms. She fought him off. "Now, Ruth," said Chuff, vexed.

"Go away!" cried Ruth in a fury. "I hate you!"

"Don't say that, Ruth," urged Chuff, beginning to be uneasy.

"I do say it. I'm disappointed in you. You're better looking since you became so sophisticated, Chuff, you talk better and hold your own better and all that. But I don't like you as I used to. You're not the boy I fell in love with. I don't want to have anything to do with you any more."

Something within Chuff felt as if it were breaking.

"For God's sake, Ruth!" he burst out fiercely. "Don't say that! Don't cut the ground from under my feet! You're the only real thing I've got left." He put his arms round her again, this time strongly.

"You old donkey, I love you, of course I do," said Ruth, weeping but fingering his shirt buttons with affection. "But you are an ass. You really are, Chuff. That girl! With all those beads and false eyelashes! How could you?"

"It was just for a bit of a change," growled Chuff. "Being so worried about the merger, and all." He did not much like the appellation of *donkey*, and felt vexed because though he had known the falsity of the eyelashes and disliked the beads from the start, it would not be very useful to say so now.

"Oh, really! Men! And what about Hal? What would be think of his father?"

Chuff at this felt the same obscure anger as on the day before. "I'm deeply sorry, Ruth," he said—soberly but not quite sincerely; he simply felt that this apology was necessary. He sighed. "I promise you it won't occur again."

"I should hope not, indeed. Well, finish your dressing," said Ruth giving his cheek a friendly pat, "or you'll be late at that mill of yours."

They exchanged a long kiss, the kiss not of passionate lovers, but of a man and wife who intend to spend their lives together. It was not indeed quite the same between them as it was before, but though in some ways less good, in others it was easier.

There were two positive results of this showdown, however. Chuff gave up his afternoon visits to Lois.

"I've come to say goodbye. This is the last time," he said with artificial cheerfulness to her, when after an absence of some weeks he entered her hall. He stood there, smiling fixedly, not taking off his coat.

Lois very naturally at once lost her temper.

"Good! I'm as tired of you as you are of me!" she shouted angrily, flushing to her throat.

"I'll leave then."

"Do."

Delighted, but feeling such a farewell, even for him, perhaps, too indecently rude, Chuff turned on the threshold, hesitated, and said again feebly, "This is the last time."

"That's right," screamed Lois. "Rub it in."

She pulled the door wide for his exit and slammed it strongly after him. Chuff rang for the lift without looking round, and went to her no more.

The other result was that a second son was born to Chuff and Ruth within the year. Ruth had a more difficult labour this time, and the child, dark like his mother, ailed a good deal in infancy, so that Chuff's pity was invoked and he felt a keen protective interest in his progress. Ruth decided that he should be named *George Cecil*, after his parents' respective fathers. Chuff did not like either name, but did not wish to hurt Ruth by vetoing them; after a while he observed that by some mysterious nursery process his second son seemed usually to be hailed as *Robin*. With this he was content.

2

A PIECE OF LUCK

IT WAS ABOUT the time when Baby Robin was struggling with whooping-cough that Chuff, entering the designing department, observed that Paul Yarrow was looking particularly ill, quite yellow. At Chuff's entrance the young man rose and left the room.

"Not after all this time, surely!" thought Chuff irritably.

"Could I have a word with you, Mr Chuff?" said old Simmonds.

Chuff nodded. They went outside on to the landing, where the subdued hum of the neighbouring loom shed throbbed warmly in their ears. Yarrow had disappeared.

"It's Paul Yarrow. He's very unhappy."

"Oh."

"Yes. His wife's left him."

"Indeed."

"Yes She's gone off with some man who teaches at the Technical College "

"He's well rid of her," said Chuff, delighted.

"He thinks he ought to leave here and take a job somewhere else and try to get her back."

"Oh, nonsense. He's doing well here. Why should he leave?"

"Well, you see, he's had the same trouble with her before. That's why he left the West of England, you see, and came North to a fresh place to give her a fresh start. What would your advice be, Mr Chuff? he is greatly troubled."

"My advice would be to stay on here, and forget her until she applies for a divorce, if ever."

"Well, I'll tell him. He's certainly doing very well here."

"How low can you get?" Chuff admonished himself as he ran downstairs. "But it's a piece of luck, so you may as well enjoy it."

3

MOTHERHOOD FOR SUSIE

"IT'S JUST AS well we have some of Uncle Harry's money," said Jonathan grimly to himself, for his expenses amounted to some three times what most assistant lecturers could afford.

The premature childbirth had hit Susie hard—she could not feed the twins herself—and it was all of two months before she was able to leave hospital. Even then, she could hardly be called able; she was weak and languid, could not walk out alone and was not in any degree fit to look after her children. Jonathan hired a trained nurse, and Susie watched quietly while the nurse bathed and dressed the twins. To care for such a household it was necessary to have some domestic help "living in", and Old Cottage really could not hold all these persons. Jonathan suggested moving into a larger house, nearer the town, and Susie seemed to agree; but one night he woke to find her sobbing by his bed—for the present, by the doctor's suggestion, they slept apart—and when he took her in his arms to comfort her, she wept out on his shoulder that she did not want to leave the cottage.

"Then we won't go," said Jonathan at once.

"Truthfully?"

"Truthfully," said Jonathan, kissing her.

He decided to add an annexe. To fight his way through architect, planning authority, builder, plumber, electrician, was a long job, and tedious to him through his inexperience; however, they were all kind to him, and the small building, of local stone and character, at length nestled snugly into the side of the cottage. To pay for it caused no difficulty. Jonathan with Susie's willing assent had arranged to place quite a sum from the sale of the Morcar shares, in a joint account in their bank, and for the annnexe and its decoration he drew on this. (The large remainder of the money he invested, by a Lorimer stockbroker's advice, in a "growth" stock—something electrical.)

After a few months the nurse began to say to Susie that it was time she learned to care for the twins; to Jonathan she urged privately that he should press this on his wife. Susie seemed to doubt whether she were capable of this exalted task, but on being reassured by her husband, undertook it with, apparently, a deep joy. Jonathan could not stay to watch the bathing ceremony in the morning, having a few miles to drive to the University; but in the evening he rushed home, and sat silent in a corner, watching with a tenderness which almost broke his heart while Susie, beaming radiantly, carefully and delicately dried those delicious small limbs. She obeyed the nurse's instructions most precisely, yet held the twins softly in her arms with all-embracing love; the infants gazed up at her and made small sounds of content. When the proceedings were over and the girls clad in their white night-attire, their eyes drowsy with sleep, Susie looked up at Jonathan, proudly and hopefully, like a child hoping for praise for a well-performed task. This praise he always gave her.

Words simply could not describe what Jonathan felt towards his children. The nurse averred she could hardly tell one daughter from the other, but though Jonathan smiled polite response, he thought this foolish; he knew them well, their appearance and their characters. Amanda was inclined to be serious, she viewed him gravely; Linda was a merry little bunch. When their hair began to grow long, like their mother's, Linda's was at all stages longer, while Amanda's had a slight curl; Amanda's eyes were soon brown, Linda's remained blue. They began to walk; Linda ran and tumbled, Amanda moved with a more cautious air. Jonathan looked forward immensely to taking his family, when Susie should be strong enough to go, to Annotsfield and showing them— yes, showing them off, he admitted gleefully—to Chuff and Ruth. Chuff did not write to Old Cottage, but it was understood that the difficulties of the merger were taxing him almost beyond endurance; Ruth wrote rather often, telling them all the news, and her invitations were frequent. But when one Christmas-time Jonathan asked Susie if she had written her acceptance to Ruth, Susie suddenly turned white, burst into tears and cried: "No! No! No!"

"I'll write then," said Jonathan hastily. It was usually he who wrote to Ruth, in fact; he liked her letters, which he found affectionate and sensible.

"No, no!" wept Susie, shuddering.

She looked quite ill, so that Jonathan was alarmed.

"Don't you want to go to Stanney Royd?"

"No. Chuff is angry with me."

"Oh, no, he isn't. Not now. He's quite forgotten all that, dear."

"I don't want to go," moaned Susie.

There was nothing for it but to yield. The situation was eased by the nurse's possession of Scottish nationality, so that she willingly sacrificed Christmas holiday for New Year. A holiday she must have, however, so Jonathan's mother, Jennifer, now for some years Mrs Nat Armitage, came to Old Cottage to stay while she was away. This did not prove successful. Susie sulked and Linda yelled. Jennifer was distressed, for she loved the little girls. She bought them beautiful frocks—Susie too—during her stay, and when she left gazed long and sorrowfully at her son as she kissed him. (The frocks were never worn.)

Another holiday period came along and Jonathan asked Susie gravely what she wished to do. Ruth was taking her children to the Yorkshire coast, would not Susie join them?

By this time Susie's health was stronger; she did not weep, but answered strongly: "No."

"What do you wish to do then?" said Jonathan, unable to prevent himself from feeling some vexation.

"I'll manage by myself, at home."

This was a step very much in the right direction, and Jonathan was glad to approve. The first morning of the nurse's absence, Susie rose early, bathed and dressed the children and was feeding them when Jonathan left for Lorimer. Delighted, he commended her highly. At night she seemed flushed and tired, but this was natural. Next day, however, Susie was still struggling in the bathroom when Jonathan left, and he had hardly reached his office when the woman who gave the Oldroyds domestic service rang to tell him drily that he had better come home at once. He rushed to the cottage.

"She won't let me touch them, Mr Oldroyd," said the woman, vexed.

Susie was sitting in the middle of the bedroom floor, a look of blank despair on her face. Linda lay in front of her, half clothed, kicking and screaming, and Amanda sat cross-legged at a distance, quietly discouraged. It appeared that Susie could not coax Linda's left arm through the sleeve of any dress. A variety of small garments, wool or nylon, lay about, with which she had made her vain attempts. Jonathan picked up the child, inserted the angrily waving little hand, and carried Linda about the room for a while against his shoulder, soothing her. When calm was restored he handed the children to the domestic, who carried them off to be fed.

"I can't do it, Jonathan. I'm so useless. I'm such a drag on you," said Susie, gazing up at him in despair.

"It's because there are two babies," said Jonathan, raising her to a chair. "One woman can't cope with two children at a time."

"Some women do. I did try."

"I know. Never mind, my darling," said Jonathan, caressing her. "I can't have you left alone without help like this. We must get another nurse."

Their first nurse was, also, becoming somewhat restless at being retained so long for patients who in her opinion no longer ought to need her; her skill would deteriorate, nurses were in short supply, and so on. Jonathan after many enquiries found a nurse slightly less skilled, but experienced, a widow anxious for a permanent job, who demanded less of life. It was at this point that Jonathan remarked to himself on the good fortune of possessing their share of the Morcar money.

"Still, it's what Uncle Harry would have wished after all, to make Susie happy," he told himself.

Now she was thus cushioned against demands too difficult for her, Susie seemed calmly happy. Jonathan bought a Mini for her, enlarging the barn which harboured the family car, to hold it, and she drove slowly about the country lanes with the twins beside her, smiling. Her smile was radiant, and it was partly this which made her so welcome, Jonathan thought, at University gatherings. She said little, but stood quietly in a corner, looking lovely—her taste in clothes was really exquisite—wearing this smile full of love and responding with wide-eyed sympathy to her neighbours' accounts of their doings and difficulties. It was true that she seemed reluctant now to entertain guests in her own home, shrinking with a look of fear when Jonathan suggested it; but his colleagues received his excuses of her ill-health kindly on this matter, and he hoped that time would heal her timidity.

The twins flourished, and Jonathan, thus domestically at peace, was able for a time to look out at the world and his function at the University.

4

YOUTH STIRS

NOT THAT THERE was much peace to be perceived in either of these spheres.

There was a terrible war of intervention, with all modern weapons except the nuclear, in Vietnam; a fearful civil war in Nigeria, a brutal disregard of human rights in South Africa and Rhodesia; an ever-looming conflict, embittered by humiliation and fear, between Israeli and Arab; violence raging and revolt preparing in the United States; oppression in Czechoslovakia; hateful, because unreasoning, propaganda in China; unease and hostility in Europe, starvation in other continents; selfishness, irresponsibility, prejudice, stupidity, everywhere.

Nor were Universities any longer places of calm learning, where the accumulated treasures of the human spirit were handed down to the coming generation. Some national authorities postulated that the training of minds had to be tailored to the national industrial need; some among students regarded a degree merely as a necessary stepping-stone to a lucrative career. Some of the most idealistic students seethed with revolt. In Germany students demonstrated their dissatisfactions with paving-stone barricades, broken windows, burnings and sackings, to which the police replied with tear-gas and water cannons. In France similar demonstrations almost brought down the De Gaulle government and forced it at least to introduce much-needed university reforms. In England, students everywhere began similar activities.

In Lorimer, these were quiet at first. A member of the Government, attending to receive an honorary degree, was treated with disapproval by students on the ground that the Cabinet of which he was a member supported the United States war in Vietnam. As he came out from the hall of the ceremony he was greeted by a group of young people of both sexes, carrying banners—home-made of poor paper, execrably printed in large uneven letters—urging the Americans to go home, to leave Vietnam alone, and so on. The sleet of an English spring was driving viciously across the draughty avenue, wilting the paper of the banners and streaming down the exposed heads and faces of the students, who stood silent and motionless, rapidly becoming soaked to the skin. Jonathan, emerging from the ceremony, grieved at this sorry spectacle at the same time as he respected its motives, and seeing a student he knew at the edge of the group, he approached him and murmured:

"Why not move about a little, to keep warm?"

To his relief, this suggestion seemed to be adopted, for in a few minutes the students began to move round, slowly and solemnly, in a small circle. Meanwhile the minister, disregarding or perhaps not even seeing his student critics, entered an official car and was driven away to lunch.

At the next meeting of the University Council—to which Jonathan, to his surprise, had recently been elected as one of the representatives of his Faculty—an elderly member brought up this business of the demonstration, complaining about the students' discourtesy to a guest, and alleging that a member of the staff, unmistakable as such because he was wearing hood and gown, had been seen instructing the demonstrating students.

"It was I who spoke to the students, sir," said Jonathan, rising at once to address the Vice-Chancellor, who was in the chair: "But the only suggestion I made to them was that they should move about. Their movement, I submit, was perfectly decorous, and they had a right to express their opinion decorously."

"Their movement made the demonstration much more noticeable and provocative," said the elderly member (who represented a town council of the district) disapprovingly.

"Why did you urge them to move, Mr Oldroyd?" enquired the Vice-Chancellor.

"I thought that if, in that very chilly sleet, they did not keep their circulation in brisk action, they might all develop pneumonia," replied Jonathan seriously.

At this there was a general titter, and even the Vice-Chancellor smiled.

No more was said about the demonstration in public, but various repercussions arose from this slight incident.

A colleague whom Jonathan disliked for his illiberal views said to him with a laugh which only half disguised a sneer:

"Be careful, Oldroyd, or your appointment won't be confirmed."

"I think better of Lorimer than that," replied Jonathan stiffly.

In the event, his three years' probation being then almost at an end, not only was he privately assured by his professor that his appointment would be confirmed, but he was also nominated to a committee appointed by the Council to consider modes of greater participation by students in University administration. This nomination he accepted very gladly.

Another, unexpected, consequence was that two or three students came up to him separately and asked whether he had thought of joining such and such a (usually left-wing political) student society. Or, sometimes they said their society had no formal membership, the meetings were open to all, they would be glad to see him there. These meetings, he noted, though usually held in the Union, sometimes took place in students' flats and sometimes even in local pubs. This discovery pointed out to him how little he knew of students' doings other than official. He longed to attend some of these meetings, for he wanted to know the size of the various groups, the identity of the members, what they thought and said. He wanted, in a word, to see more nearly the contents of the minds he was supposed to guide and nourish.

Particularly did he yearn for this after one of his students, a rather dull but earnest and well-meaning lad, threw himself off the roof of one of the incomplete new buildings to meet a suicide's death below. His friends said he had been taking tranquillisers for weeks, as he was terribly troubled by the approach of examinations.

"Tranquillisers!" exclaimed Jonathan, horrified.

The students looked at him pityingly; taking tranquillisers was obviously a familiar ploy to them. Jonathan had not, fortunately for his peace of mind, been guilty of snubbing or severely criticising the unhappy lad, but still he sorrowed.

"If only he had come to me! But what could I have said to him, after all? If only I knew them better! There are too many!"

The boy's blank, discouraged face, fair and flaccid, scarred with the blemishes of adolescence, haunted him.

But he did not feel able to leave Susie two or three nights every week; he could not withdraw so often the support she required. He had observed all too clearly how much more cheerful she was in the holidays, when he was with her all the time.

"I'm afraid I can't come at present," he replied mildly to

the enquiring students. "I can't undertake any further evening outgoings, at present."

At this, students who had seen the beautiful Susie about and by chance knew her identity, leered; the others wore a look of disappointment and contempt. It could not be helped.

5

SUSIE DEFEATED

ONE MORNING AS Jonathan was lecturing he was interrupted by the secretary of the Department, who entered the room in a hurry with a look of trouble. It was Jonathan's firm intention to show discourtesy to no human being, but he could not help a look of some vexation; he cherished his lecture periods and disliked to have one spoiled. Advancing swiftly to him the girl said in a low voice in his ear that the Lorimer police had rung the Department. It seemed that Mr Oldroyd's wife had been involved in a motoring irregularity and they would be grateful if he would go at once to the central police station.

Jonathan with a look of horror stammered a few words of excuse to his audience and rushed away.

He sprang up the steps of the police station, seized upon the uniformed man at the reception desk, and was ushered into a small empty room, where presently a tall solid handsome man in uniform, whom from his insignia Jonathan vaguely recognised as possibly the Chief Constable, came in and greeted him.

"Mr Oldroyd? We were sorry to disturb you during University hours, but thought it wise to summon you."

"What has happened? Is my wife hurt?" cried Jonathan, wild with anxiety.

"No. She is physically quite unharmed."

The word *physically* struck a knell on Jonathan's ear. Inwardly he trembled, but controlled himself to say more soberly:

"I have no idea what has happened. Is it a car accident?"

"Not exactly an accident."

"For heaven's sake," burst out Jonathan: "Tell me what is wrong."

"We were summoned by the branch manager," said the Chief Constable, naming a large multiple firm. "At the side of the store there is a narrow passage-way expanding into a small courtyard with an unloading bay used by their vans. Drivers found their way blocked by a small private car. They approached to ask for it to be moved, and found at the wheel Mrs Oldroyd, weeping and distracted."

"Ah," breathed Jonathan.

"She was quite incapable of handling her car."

"Where is she now?"

"The manager telephoned us and an inspector and a woman police constable went to the store and brought the car and Mrs Oldroyd here to the station. She made no resistance but declined to drive her car herself."

"Since nobody was hurt and no damage was done, I presume I am at liberty to take her home at once. No doubt there will be a fine, which I will, of course, pay at once."

"We took a breathalyser test," said the Chief Constable quietly.

"My wife and I do not drink, sir," said Jonathan, furious.

"Mr Oldroyd, our police doctor assures us that your wife is not in a fit state to drive a car."

"I will take further advisement on that."

"If we could have your assurance that she will not drive at present," began the Chief Constable. "Otherwise it will mean an endorsement of her licence, perhaps even a long suspension, a ban, in Court."

Jonathan stared at him.

"Mr Oldroyd," continued the older man in a grave but kindly tone: "To speak unofficially: with the greatest respect, your wife is in need of care and attention."

"I give her all possible care and attention," blurted Jonathan, his face contorting.

There was a pause.

"Take me to her."

He followed the Chief Constable along dreary stone passages and up stone stairways to a comfortable carpeted little room warmed by a gas-fire, which he guessed to be the Chief Constable's own apartment. There sat Susie crouched in a chair, a woman constable beside her. A half-drunk cup of tea stood cold on a corner of the desk. Susie's face was white, her lips quivered, large tears stood in her starry eyes, she stared blankly. But as usual she looked exquisitely, touchingly beautiful, and there was a look of affectionate pity on the policewoman's face.

"Here's your husband, Mrs Oldroyd," she said brightly.

Susie looked up, intelligence lighted her eyes and she cried: "Jonathan! Jonathan!"

Jonathan knelt beside her and took her in his arms.

"I can't do it, Jonathan. I can't do it! I can't!" cried Susie, burying her face in his shoulder and sobbing wildly.

"What can't you do, my darling?"

"I can't drive in the town. It's too difficult. All those signs, and double yellow lines, and cars rushing about, coming out suddenly, and traffic policemen and one-way streets, and so many rules, I can't remember them. I can't do it. I was frightened. I went down that lane to be safe, to be out of it all."

"Well, never mind. There's no need for you to drive a car if you don't want to," said Jonathan consolingly.

"But how shall we manage? We have to shop. I can't do it. I dream about it," wept Susie.

"Goodness me! We can't have you upsetting yourself like that. I can do the shopping. I'll think it out. I'll plan it. Don't you worry any more."

"You're so good to me, Jonathan," said Susie, gazing up at him gratefully.

He kissed the tears from her pale cheeks, and the police-woman, smiling with relief, brought two more cups of tea.

On their way home from the police station, Susie mur-mured: "You won't tell Chuff about this, will you?"

Jonathan gave his promise.

A doctor, of course, had to be consulted. Summoned on the following day, when Susie had grown calmer, he put in a strong plea for the services of a psychiatrist.

"What's the use of psycho-analysis in this case?" said Jonathan. "We already know the trauma which caused her mental disturbance."

He explained about the murder of Susie's parents.

"They were killed in some kind of race disturbance, in South Africa," he said. "I don't know the exact details. The bodies were—mangled—and Susie unfortunately saw them."

"Ah," said the doctor: "A severe shock."

"She's just not equal to the stress of modern life. Heaven knows it is almost unbearable," he said.

"Nevertheless," began the doctor, a youngish man of modern ideas.

"I shall guard her most carefully from all troubles and worries."

"It's not enough. She needs treatment."

"She clings to me. If you separate us the result may be disastrous."

"I should like to put the suggestion of treatment to her, all the same," said the doctor obstinately.

"If you feel it is essential, of course I cannot refuse, but I dread the effect on my wife."

They returned to the bedroom where Susie lay looking fragile against her pillows.

"We have been discussing the idea of treatment for you, Mrs Oldroyd, to help you feel more confident," said the doctor in a soothing professional tone.

Susie shrank, and looked up in appeal at Jonathan.

"If you think I must," she said faintly.

"Good. And you'll be willing to go away from home for a little while to receive it, won't you?"

"No, no!" cried Susie, her cheek blanching and her eyes dilating with fear. "Jonathan! Don't let me go!" She seized her husband's arm and clung to it with all her might.

"Of course you shan't go if you don't want to," said Jonathan cheerfully. "That is so, isn't it, Doctor?"

"Of course, of course," agreed the doctor. "It was just a suggestion. Good morning, Mrs Oldroyd. Stay in bed and rest, and I will call again and see how you are, tomorrow."

Outside the room he said to Jonathan: "I apologise. You know your wife better than I do, of course. But she may change her mind. If she doesn't improve she may come to wish for treatment. If she does, we must take advantage of it at once."

There followed a twelvemonth when Susie's mental health continually deteriorated. This sad progress was intermittent. Sometimes it went slowly, with periods of recovery, sometimes by leaps and bounds. She looked at her daughters, for instance, sometimes with conscious love, sometimes with a sweet but unrecognising smile. The days when she had driven a car and gone out to parties began to seem far away and long ago. The doctor continued to urge electrical and other treatment. Jonathan shrank from it.

"You know, Mr Oldroyd," said the doctor to him one day: "This may be very painful to you, but the truth is—or rather, the truth may be—that your wife is beginning to feel guilty and ineffective towards you too."

"Oh, no!" said Jonathan, struck to the heart. He hesitated,

then added: "She is more likely to feel guilt towards her brother."

The doctor gave him a look which meant: *You are inventing this: it is a rationalisation.*

Jonathan fought against this judgment, for if Susie could no longer rest absolutely upon him, surely she would indeed despair. He took all possible pains to show her how great was his love and desire for her, how happy he was to come home and find her by his hearth, how greatly he admired her beauty, her taste, her soft little voice. He talked to her, carefully and simply, of events in the University and the outside world, to show how highly he valued her intelligence and opinion. But Susie certainly did not improve.

At last there came an evening when, sitting at the supper-table with her husband—he had been talking about Vietnam—and picking up a fork in the customary way, she suddenly appeared to forget what it was and why she held it, and stared blankly at the implement in her hand.

"Susie!" exclaimed Jonathan. (In spite of himself alarm and anguish crept into his voice.)

Susie returned to herself and employed the fork normally. But in a moment she said in her soft sweet tones:

"I'll have some treatment, Jonathan, if you think it will make me better."

"And will you—go away—to have it?" said Jonathan, his words sticking in his throat.

Susie sighed. "Yes, if I must," she said mildly.

It was arranged, and she entered the institution the following day.

Jonathan, with leaden heart and outward cheer, visited her as often as the institute doctors would allow; he had thought of taking the children, now nearly four years old, to see her once a week, but the doctors advised against it.

Perhaps this was fortunate, for within ten days another

blow fell. Mrs Willoughby, the widow who had made whatever comfort had existed in their home for the last few years,
came to him weeping and handed in her notice. It appeared
that her daughter's youngest boy had developed polio, and
her aid was needed in nursing him.

"Of course you must go at once, Mrs Willoughby," said
Jonathan, sick at heart. "But what I shall do without you, I
don't know."

"I hope you think I've done my duty by you, Mr Oldroyd."

"I do indeed."

"It hasn't always been easy, with Mrs Oldroyd as she is,
and that."

"I fully appreciate your great services, Mrs Willoughby,"
said Jonathan, giving her a handsome present.

"What will you do with the two poor mites?" pursued
Mrs Willoughby.

"Until Mrs Oldroyd returns," began Jonathan.

"Ah!" said Mrs Willoughby shaking her head.

"I think I must put them in the care of their aunt,"
concluded Jonathan, thinking with a rush of relief of Ruth's
homely warmth.

"Yes. Your mother's a bit tired for two such young ones,"
agreed Mrs Willoughby.

"If you can just find time to pack for them before you
go, I shall be grateful."

Mrs Willoughby ironed out a slight frown at this suggestion and found time to perform this service.

On the following Saturday Jonathan put the twins into
his car and drove to Stanney Royd.

6

TWO DAUGHTERS

ROBIN HAD RECOVERED from two or three infantile ailments and become able to toddle when one Saturday morning Chuff by chance reached home rather early. He has just received the second half of his income tax demand and was feeling bad-tempered; still, there would be golf in the afternoon. As he dismounted from his car he saw a small fair sprite watching him with great interest from the nearby rockery. The very fair long hair, the charming short little shift which children wore nowadays, her white socks and shoes, made her a delicious sight, to which Chuff was not unsusceptible.

"Well now, who are *you*?" he said, smiling and extending a hand to her. The sprite with a radiant smile skipped over the rockery and confided her small paw to his. They advanced along the side of the house. Ruth came out of the front door, looking rather harassed. At her side, but not holding her hand, stood another sprite almost identical with the first, except that her little white shift was starred with blue roses, whereas his sprite's had pink.

'Who are these, then?' called Chuff laughing.

"They're Susie's twins, of course," said Ruth. "This is Amanda, yours is Linda. Amanda's a few minutes older."

"They're raving beauties," exclaimed Chuff with satisfaction.

"What did you expect?" snapped Ruth. "They're Susie's children."

Chuff held out his hand to Amanda. She did not move, but gazed at him with disapproval. He now observed that she was slightly less pretty, though perhaps more beautiful than her sister, for her forehead was higher and the dressing of her fair silky hair, tied back rather severely on top of her head with a black ribbon, made her profile appear rather austere.

"Is Susie here, then?" said Chuff.

"No, Jonathan brought them. Don't say anything, Chuff. Twins, run along to Mrs Jessopp and tell her Uncle Chuff is here."

The sprites vanished obediently.

"I must say I think Jonathan and Susie might have accepted our holiday invitations and brought them here before," said Chuff.

"We shall have to keep them, Chuff, at any rate for a while," whispered Ruth, taking his arm.

"What do you mean?"

"Susie's had to go into a nursing home."

"Well, they might have told us sooner. What's wrong?"

"A nervous breakdown."

"You don't mean——" began Chuff, halting suddenly.

"Yes, I'm afraid I do. She's never been herself since they were born, you know, and now she's broken down completely."

"Susie!"

"Jonathan's here—he'll tell you about it. Or perhaps he won't," said Ruth. "Don't press him too hard."

Her face contorted and she appeared near to tears. From Ruth, who was not given to displays of emotion, this was serious.

"We'll keep the twins as long as necessary," she said unevenly.

"Of course," said Chuff.

7

DISAGREEMENTS

THE TWO COUSINS gazed at each other in astonishment. From a series of apparently trivial causes which sprang from deep divisions, they had not seen each other since the night of the twins' birth, and each perceived startling changes in the other.

To Chuff, Jonathan, though only in his early thirties, looked a man in middle life, and a worn man at that. For he was thin to emaciation, greying at the temples, his face haggard, deeply lined. His eyes still shone, but no longer with ardent life; they were the eyes of a man who had learned strength through grief.

Chuff, on the other hand, appeared to Jonathan not only exceedingly sleek and well groomed, but almost handsome. Lines round his mouth showed sophistication, and his eyes had lost their boyish frankness. He held himself well and walked with confidence. In a word, he had grown up.

"Chuff!" exclaimed Jonathan, smiling and offering his hand.

"Long time no see," said Chuff, taking it. "What will you have to drink?"

"Nothing, thanks."

"Well, sit down anyway," said Chuff, mixing himself a rather strong whisky and soda—seeing Jonathan look so old had upset him. "I'm sorry to hear this about Susie. It's not —permanent, is it?"

"No, no. Just a few weeks. Perhaps a month or two. I should be very grateful if you could keep the twins until she's well enough to return home. Mrs Willoughby has had to leave, you see, owing to illness in her own family, and term is just beginning, so I am not free. But if it should be troublesome to Ruth, I'm sure Mother——"

"The place of Susie's children is here," said Chuff firmly.

At this point the elder twin ran in, and took up her position by her father's knee, leaning one arm across him with a protective air.

"This one's Amanda?"

"Yes." Jonathan gently stroked the child's gleaming head. "They're very like Susie, don't you think?"

"Yes and no," said Chuff, who personally read in Amanda's defiant little face a likeness to Jonathan which intimidated him.

Ruth, holding Linda's hand, with Hal and Robin skirmishing on the sidelines, now entered to announce that lunch was ready. Linda—what a beauty that child is! thought Chuff—glided across to her father and took his extended hand.

"Who are those?" said Hal, pointing.

"Don't point, dear," said his mother. "Those are your cousins Amanda and Linda; their mother is ill, so we are looking after them for a while."

"Oh," said Hal, his face slightly softening. "They look like dolls."

"We'll go to Annotsfield this afternoon and buy them some dolls," suggested Ruth.

Hal appeared to consider this *non sequitur* doubtfully. Robin drew near the twins. He stood and gazed at them, his hands clasped over his thin little stomach, but said nothing.

Lunch, with four young children present, was a meal messy and often interrupted. Jonathan was used to this and took it calmly, but Chuff, he noticed with some surprise, was irritable and impatient.

In the intervals of tears, spoon-feeding, refusals to eat and mopping up mouths and bibs, Ruth contrived to ask:

"But what do you *do* at a University, Jonathan?"

Jonathan explained the preparation and delivery of lectures—he had two courses this year—tutorials, the return of essays and so on; they listened in awe.

"Return the compliment, Chuff, and tell us what you do."

"I can't describe it all," said Chuff sulkily. "We design cloth and weave it, Hamsun's other subsidiaries finish it and the group markets it."

"It's in the design you miss Uncle Harry most, I expect," said Jonathan wanting to show interest.

"Yes."

Something in the haste of this curt answer, and an odd look on Ruth's face, showed Jonathan that the subject was unwelcome; he bent over Linda and adjusted her "pusher".

Afterwards Ruth took the children away and the two men sat alone together over coffee.

"I should like to say again how deeply I regretted the affair of the Morcar shares," said Jonathan in a formal tone. "As I told you at the time, I knew nothing of it till after the sale was completed."

"Oh—it proved a good thing out of a bad one," said Chuff carelessly.

Jonathan felt chilled, but he persevered, determined to show concern for his cousin's affairs.

"There's a City Takeover Panel now, isn't there? Didn't the Government tighten it up a bit recently?"

"I daresay. I have nothing to complain about in our takeover," said Chuff as before. He hesitated, rather wanting to tell how he had tried to protect the interests of the Daisy Mill men, but he decided he was too proud to seek his cousin's approval, and said nothing.

There was a silence. Jonathan broke it by saying with forced cheerfulness:

"How is G.B.?"

"We haven't seen him lately. He went to a job in London."

"Electronics?"

"No. Trade Union. But now he's got into Parliament, you know. The previous member conveniently died."

"Is he Trade Union sponsored?"

"Don't mention Trades Unions to me. More than four million work hours lost through strikes this year already! Did you ever hear anything like it? With our adverse trade balance!"

"Perhaps the Trades Unions are not the only ones to blame—it may not be altogether their fault," suggested Jonathan mildly.

"Well, it's not mine," snapped Chuff. With an effort he recalled his temper and said more pleasantly: "G.B. doesn't write to Ruth, but he writes to his mother pretty regularly, I believe, and we hear his news that way. He's only called in here once since he left Annotsfield. He looked very prosperous."

"There has been a general rise in the standard of living, rather than a better distribution of wealth, I think," said Jonathan stiffly.

"That's what *you* think. We always did disagree. What do you think about these student riots, then, eh?"

"I regard these protesting University students as one of the hopes of the century," said Jonathan, losing his temper in his turn.

Chuff's eyes opened so wide, in such horror, at this sentiment, that Jonathan repented. He laughed and added: "At least sometimes I do so."

"And sometimes not, I hope."

"Well, I must be off. I must call to see Mother," said Jonathan. He rose, feeling that further talk would only bring further disagreement.

Chuff, who agreed with him on this point, did not try to detain him.

The parting between Jonathan and his children was agonising. Linda screamed and sobbed till her little face lost all its beauty in crimson distortion; she clung to her father with all her strength. When Chuff lifted her away and raised her to his shoulder, she beat at him with clenched fists; Chuff however, retained her in his arms, he felt curiously drawn to this convulsive resentful little organism. Meanwhile Amanda stood motionless, pale and silent. Her parting embrace with her father was long but without sound. For his part Jonathan felt as if some ruthless god were digging out his heart with a sharp grape-fruit spoon. He was obliged to pause for several minutes at the entrance to the drive of Emsley Hall, to regain his composure and put on a cheerful countenance.

"Mr Jonathan, madam," announced the old Armitage retainer who had lived at Emsley Hall since Nat was an infant.

The Armitages were sitting comfortably in armchairs on either side of their enormous hearth. The furnishings of the huge room were (in Jonathan's opinion) hideously Victorian, dating from the 1870's when a former Armitage, profiting by the distress of French textile firms after the Franco-German War, added enormously to a fortune already two hundred years old, and redecorated the Hall.

His mother tried to start up to greet him, but the stick she had recently taken to using slipped from her reach and she sank back. Nat rose and shook his stepson warmly by the hand.

"Jonathan! Why didn't you let us know you were coming,

dear? Is Susie with you? Have you brought the twins?"

Nerving himself to an ordeal he dreaded, Jonathan bent over his mother and kissed her still handsome cheek, then explained calmly:

"I'm sorry to say Susie is not very well and has had to go into a nursing home for a spell. I have brought the children over to spend a few weeks with Chuff and Ruth."

"What is the matter with Susie?"

"A kind of nervous breakdown, I'm afraid."

"Oh, Jonathan!" mourned his mother. She gazed at him sorrowfully. "You're not looking at all well, Jonathan."

"I can't say the same of you," returned Jonathan in a sprightly tone.

This was the merest truth; his mother's blonde hair was slightly greying, but its handsome dressing displayed its abundance, her grey eyes were bright, her fair complexion unblemished. Life as Nat Armitage's wife was clearly easy for her, thought Jonathan with a pang of perhaps jealousy, perhaps envy.

"I'll just pop off and write a letter or two, Jennifer, and then you two can have a heart to heart talk," said Nat with his customary friendly courtesy. "You'll stay for a cuppa, I suppose, Jonathan?"

He waved a valedictory hand and left them.

"Oh, Jonathan! A nervous breakdown! I always knew that would happen in some form or another," grieved Jennifer. "Susie was always unstable, Jonathan, you could see it as well as I could. Everyone saw it—your Uncle Harry saw it clearly, though he was so fond of her. Why did you ever marry her?"

"Mother, I love Susie," said Jonathan.

He did not have to pretend to make this statement; it was the merest truth and it carried conviction. His mother sighed.

"And the twins! Why didn't you bring them to me, Jonathan?"

This was not quite so easy to explain.

"They would be too much for you, Mother, nowadays—with your rheumatism," said Jonathan. He could hardly say that he had thought Ruth would be a more yielding and cheerful hostess than his mother. "They're very active little minxes, you know—they gallop about all over the place all the time," he finished on a descending note.

His mother was not deceived. Her lips quivered and her eyes filled with tears. "Your father's grandchildren, Jonathan," she murmured.

Jonathan, a posthumous child who knew his father only from photographs of him in parachutist uniform, now through his own experience of married love, understood his mother's feelings much more clearly than he had done as a boy.

"I'm sorry, Mother," he said gently. "But Chuff, you see, is Susie's brother."

There was a pause.

"Ruth will be kind to them," he added.

"Oh, Ruth will be good to them," agreed his mother. "Ruth is a good girl, kind and warm-hearted. But as for Chuff, that's a different matter. Chuff has changed very much of late years. Chuff treated Nat very badly over the takeover.'

"Surely not," protested Jonathan.

"Oh yes, he did. He didn't obtain a seat on the Hamsun Board for Nat, you know—never even asked for one."

Jonathan was silent; he felt there might be another version of this affair.

"Could you perhaps arrange with Ruth for her to bring the twins up here for tea one afternoon a week regularly? Every Wednesday for instance, or Saturday perhaps when I could be here. That would be a good way to keep in touch and not too demanding," suggested Jonathan, trying as always to find a friendly solution to a problem.

In this case he seemed successful, for his mother's face brightened.

'That's a good idea. I'll telephone her. I'll ring her now, shall I?"

"Why not?" said Jonathan encouragingly.

Jennifer went to the telephone, but returned looking disappointed.

"She's out," she said. (Jonathan remembered the projected Annotsfield expedition in search of dolls.) "But I'll ring her tonight. I'd rather the twins came alone, you know—I mean, without Chuff's boys. Hal is a very rough little boy, and Robin is always ailing."

"I'm sure it can be arranged," said Jonathan soothingly.

But he sighed to find family enmities rising around the children almost before they could talk.

8

"THE WOOL IS RISING"

"HOW DO THEY contrive to arrange their hair in these apparently careless waves which yet make an agreeable pattern?" wondered Jonathan, observing the well-shaped dark head in front of him, bent downward as the young man, freshman student this term, nervously ruffled the pages of his essay to find a criticised passage. "I suppose they contrive it as Lord Byron contrived it," he reflected with some amusement. "Rebels always contrive this carefully dishevelled hair. It's symptomatic. I suppose it expresses their revolt against convention—yes, of course it does. The waves are arranged, all the same—it's another convention. I presume you are studying for the degree of Bachelor of Arts in General Studies, Mr Mellor?" he said aloud, and seeing by the lad's face that it was so, continued: "What subjects are you taking?"

"Economics, history and English."

"It is economics which chiefly interest you."

"Of course."

"Yes, I have observed that you can't write an essay on any literary subject without providing some economic interpretation."

"The economic interpretation exists in the text!" flashed the student, his rather small black eyes brightening to an eager glow.

"Even if the writer didn't intend it?"

"All the more then."

"You have a point there," conceded Jonathan. "But, my dear fellow, your desire for an economic interpretation must not be allowed to lead you into inaccuracies. For instance, in this essay you have implied that Emily Brontë had, even if unconsciously, communist leanings, because it is springtime at the end of *Wuthering Heights*, springtime when the new is growing and the old is dead."

"It's a legitimate symbolism, surely."

"But it is not springtime at the end of *Wuthering Heights*. The season is autumn."

"No! Stocks and wallflowers are in bloom. Mr Lockwood catches their scent on his last visit to the Heights."

"Stocks and wallflowers begin to bloom in the spring, but continue throughout the summer. Heather, however, does not bloom till late August or early September, and heather is blooming on the three graves of Cathy, Edgar and Heathcliff, when Mr Lockwood visits them that night."

The student looked considerably abashed, but suddenly recovered.

"I don't believe the heather is blooming, sir; heath is mentioned, but not that it's in flower."

"Let us examine the passage."

They opened the copies of the novel they respectively held. Jonathan's his own, the student's from a municipal library.

"I believe you are right, Mr Mellor," said Jonathan gravely. "*Heath* is mentioned without reference to flowers, and *harebells* seem to clinch the matter—though I don't know for certain when harebells bloom. Do you?"

"I live in the city of Lorimer, sir," said the boy with bitterness.

"We must look up harebells. I don't believe Emily had views in your sense, however. Her spirit could not have been chained to any narrow political creed."

"She could have been an anarchist," said the boy, his eyes glowing.

"That is possible. Give some thought to that then with

special reference to her poetry, *The Philosopher* you know, and *Ay, there it is* and of course, *No Coward Soul.*"

The young man groaned.

"Did you track down that ungrammatical sentence I spoke of? It came towards the end," said Jonathan, holding out his hand for the essay, as he guessed that the student did not recognise the error to which he referred. "Here it is— you've allowed an unattached, or perhaps I should say, wrongly attached participle to stray into your prose. *Having thus set Hareton and Catherine on the road to love, Heathcliff has come to his time to die.* Do you really mean that Heathcliff set the cousins on the road to love?"

"No, of course not."

"Then don't say so. Present and past participles must be attached to a noun. If you analyse the sentence—but I forgot; analysis is not taught in schools nowadays."

"No," said Mellor defiantly.

"By the way," said Jonathan, as the student inserted the essay pages into his loose-leaf folder, "I am interested in your name."

To his surprise a dark burning blush suffused the sallow cheeks of the young man.

"How did you know I had no right to it?"

"I hadn't the slightest idea!" disclaimed Jonathan, blushing in his turn with shame for his *gaffe*. "I do apologise if I have trespassed on your private affairs. Mellor is a frequent name in the West Riding, of course—this may be just a coincidence—but my grandmother was a Mellor, and she had a father named Charles and a younger brother named David—who was killed early in the 1914 War. Your initials, C.D.—Charles David?—I just wondered—pure coincidence, no doubt."

"My name is Charles David, but I've no right to the name of Mellor, in law," said Mellor angrily. "At least, I suppose not."

Jonathan looked attentive.

"My father was illegitimate. Son of a soldier, killed in 1914, who hadn't time to marry his girl before he was sent off to the front. She took his name, though, right or wrong, and registered the child under it, and we've stuck to it ever since."

"An uncomfortable story. But I don't suppose your father is troubled by it nowadays," said Jonathan soothingly.

"No, but I am!" flashed Mellor. "Just another example of the glories of war."

"Indeed, yes. My grandmother's elder brother has descendants. One of them is married to my half-cousin," said Jonathan, who felt that a spate of talk might gloss over and carry them through this awkward moment. (At the same time he thought of Ruth and his daughters, and suffered a pang.) "The other, G. B. Mellor, has recently won a seat for Labour—you may have heard of him."

"Those old fossils!" exclaimed Mellor with contempt. "None of them are less than fifty."

"G. B. Mellor is barely forty, I believe," said Jonathan crisply.

"It's all the same. Their minds are like concrete—set in the mould of 1883."

"No doubt every generation feels the same about the previous generation," said Jonathan, appreciating, however, Mellor's knowledge of the date when the Weavers' Guild, the first textile trade union, was founded. "I know nothing of the history of my grandmother's younger brother, David, I'm afraid, so I don't know whether I'm entitled to claim relationship with you, presuming you're his grandson, or not."

Mellor hesitated, and the look of anger on his face melted into one of mischief.

"I've always hoped I was descended from the Luddite murderer of 1812," he said defiantly.

"Indeed! I almost certainly am descended from him," said Jonathan.

"Really?"

"Yes, really."

"Why don't you come to our Anarchist meetings, sir? We should be pleased to have you. If you're a murderous Mellor, you should be on our side."

"I have other ancestors," said Jonathan stiffly.

"So it seems from your name. How do you come to be an Oldroyd?"

"It's a long story," said Jonathan as before, resenting on his father's behalf—for the first time in his life, perhaps—the contempt for all Oldroyds revealed in Mellor's tone. "You say *our side*. What does that imply?"

"Revolt!"

"Against what?"

"Everything! We want to shake the pillars which uphold the riddle of the world!"

"Malraux," said Jonathan, recognising the quotation from *Antimémoires*.

Mellor looked a trifle disconcerted, as if unpleasantly surprised to find somebody else—a lecturer at that—as well versed in "left" readings as himself.

"Malraux isn't a revolutionary nowadays," he said, clearly intending to deprive Jonathan of credit for reading him. "He's a minister under de Gaulle."

"True. He has a right to modify his views if he wishes."

Mellor made a sound of contempt. "And we have the right to disapprove."

"Of course; but freedom of thought and speech does not mean only freedom for one's own side," said Jonathan.

"The pillars want shaking all the same! And you are going to hear a great deal more of us doing it. *The Wool is Rising*," said Mellow ominously.

"I see you've been reading Branwell Brontë," said Jonathan, unable not to feel pleased by this citing of the title of an obscure day-dream writing of the Brontë brother. "You are interested in Branwell, perhaps?"

"He was in revolt," said Mellor with passion.

"An ineffective life, however. The Billy Liar of his century."

"I do *wish* you would come to our meetings, Mr Oldroyd," said Mellor in a tone almost of pleading.

Jonathan waited for him to say that the lecturer might have something to contribute to the meetings, but this did not come, so he said sardonically:

"You think it would do me good? Set me on the right track?"

"Well, yes," said Mellor, laughing.

"Perhaps you would care to compile a few notes on a comparison of the ethics of Branwell and Emily Brontë," said Jonathan drily.

Mellor went out looking pleased with himself.

Looking back at this interview, Jonathan was dissatisfied with his part in it. He had sounded, he thought, essentially as a member of a previous generation sounded to a present one—reactionary, unaware, with a closed mind, interested only in unimportant and outdated trivia. Mellor on the other hand, though vigorous and idealistic, was jejune and uninformed.

Jonathan debated with himself whether to attend a meeting of Mellor's cherished group. Heaven knew there was nothing on his cold and lonely hearth now to keep him at home in the evenings. His hesitation concluded a few days later when there appeared in huge white letters (very unshapely) on the wall of a Lorimer University building, the slogan: THE SYSTEM IS ROTTEN DESTROY IT. He smiled to himself to observe that the youthful anarchists had

not defaced a new building, but kindly—or perhaps sym-
bolically—vented their wrath on an old one. But it was time,
he thought, that somebody suggested to these young hot-
heads the advisability of planning another system to take its
place, before proceeding to destroy the one, however imper-
fect, at present working—he had gathered from Mellor that
the present mild form of Welfare State was as much despised
as capitalism.

He glanced at the Union notice board to mark the
relevant day and time, and presently found himself sitting on
the floor—the bed was full—against the wall in a student's
chilly, meagrely furnished private room, surrounded by some
score of (he presumed) anarchical revolutionaries of both
sexes. The walls, agreeably free from female pin-ups,
featured instead newspaper portraits of Mao, Che Guevara
and Daniel Cohn-Bendit in characteristically defiant atti-
tudes. A youth who stammered seemed to be host; there
were no other members of faculty present.

"Is it true that you and Mellor are related?" said a girl in
long black network stockings, sitting beside him, abruptly.

"We are not certain, but there are some grounds for
supposing so."

Mellor, who seemed to be in the chair, now made an
admirable speech, laying his finger firmly on all the miseries
of the contemporary scene: the wars, the injustices, the
starvation, the oppression, the maldistribution of wealth, the
nuclear weapons, immigration. He was received with fervent
applause and enthusiastic cries of approval. A girl next
delivered a passionate indictment of American behaviour in
Vietnam, and a third student delivered an amusingly
satiric description of the doings of the present British
Government. Ireland, the Pope, of course the Pill, voyages
to the moon and University curricula were argued over, and
finally the meeting condescended to discuss weekend leave.

The ability displayed came down the scale as the meeting meeting went on, but shot up when the Vietnam war came again on the agenda. The main speakers all spoke well, even with eloquence, and knew their facts; it was by no means a display of "blind and naked Ignorance" delivering "brawling judgments". The only point indeed on which Jonathan strongly disagreed was the vehement accusation of specific persons and organisations for deliberate wrongdoings, rather than a general deploring such as he would have favoured, of human ignorance, human inability (as yet) to think out solutions.

"Perhaps Mr Oldroyd would like to say a word to us about peace," said Mellor suddenly.

"Clever of him to choose the least controversial topic on which to call me in," thought Jonathan, rising; and caught thus unawares he threw out the sentence which expressed one of his most profound convictions: "*If we would have peace without a worm in it, lay we foundations of justice and righteousness.*"

There was silence.

"Who said that?" demanded Mellor at length in a disagreeable tone.

"Oliver Cromwell."

"Is C-C-Cromwell a f-f-favourite of yours?" demanded the youth who stammered badly.

"No. Fairfax is my man. How do you feel about Cromwell?"

"Look how he p-p-put down the Levellers," continued the youth. "He chased them away from the Army and shot one dead. He was against p-p-power until he got it, and then he liked it and used it without mercy."

"It's all too common a fault," said Jonathan drily, reflecting that a First Year History course must have reached the Civil War, for badly though the lad stammered, his facts emerged correctly. "Look at all revolutionaries of modern times."

"Let us take Power as our next week's theme," suggested Mellor brightly.

"An excellent choice," approved Jonathan.

Having said this, he felt a certain moral obligation to be present at the next week's discussion. He promised himself to be silent unless directly called upon, but after a raging speech in favour of violent demonstrations from the black-stockinged girl—who it appeared was Mellor's girl friend; they were possibly sleeping together, but of course, Jonathan did not enquire into this—he felt obliged to intervene.

"I don't support your equation of power with violence and physical force," he said.

"You can't do anything without power," said the girl.

"There I agree. Knowledge, goodwill and power—in the sense of determination and freedom to reform—are the three prerequisites of any useful reforming action."

"All p-p-power is b-b-based on f-f-force," said the stammerer.

"The base is a long way down," observed Jonathan, smiling.

"You are obliged to use violence if you want anybody to take any notice of you," said the girl hotly.

"If you support that view you are supporting American action in Vietnam and Russian action in Czechoslovakia," said Jonathan.

This Russian reference was ill-received. So much so, in fact, that after the close of the meeting, Jonathan hung back for an opportunity to say to Mellor:

"If my interventions are disagreeable to your members, I will gladly stay away from the meetings. But I can't come to the meetings and remain silent. I must protest against what I believe to be wrong."

"Oh, they don't object to you," replied Mellor cheerfully. "They think it sharpens their wits to have somebody to argue with."

After this Jonathan's term seemed to consist, apart from his Saturday meetings with the twins at Emsley Hall, in discussions with Mellor, which too often sprang away from literature and ranged throughout the universe, including heaven and hell. The two subjects which seriously concerned all the students at the time were curricula and participation in University government. Mellor had much to say on both.

"What objections have you to the present English course, Mr Mellor?" enquired Jonathan on an essay-returning occasion.

"The whole system's wrong!" began Mellor, at the top of his voice.

"Don't shout at me as if I were a public meeting. Let us discuss the matter quietly, as rational members of a civilisation."

"But there's no civilisation about it. University is supposed to give us the entry to civilisation, a participation in culture, a sharing in cultural excitement, a response to it. But we don't get any such thing. These stupid examinations lead us up the garden! Not that it's a garden; it's the dreariest kind of desert."

"But do you deserve a cultural garden?"

"Why not? Everyone deserves it! If you mean because of class——" began Mellor hotly.

"No, no, no. But if you don't understand, say *Paradise Lost*, or find Meredith meaningless, you think it's the University's fault."

"Well, whose fault is it if not the University's?"

"Largely yours."

"I don't agree," said Mellor with passion. "We ask bread, and are given a stone, that's what I say."

"You're not willing to make an effort, to work to

understand. Let me ask you a question: did you look up the blooming period of harebells?"

"I can't waste time on such a trivial bourgeois detail," said Mellor sulkily.

"But it was essential to the correct interpretation of Emily Brontë—or at any rate, to your interpretation of her thought."

Mellor was silent.

"Did *you* look it up?" he said at length roughly.

"Yes. Let's see, I wrote it down somewhere," said Jonathan, drawing out his engagement diary. "At the back here. Yes: *It displays its blue bell-shaped flowers during July to September*. A rather thicker kind, with different leaves *throws up its racemes of blue bells during a late season (September and October)*. But as that kind grows in woods and copses, I don't think it's Emily's. The first kind *thrives on pastures and on dry heaths*. Dry heaths are Emily's, I think. But you can't call July to September springtime, can you? Two other authorities say it flowers *July to September*, that is summer and early autumn. On the other hand wallflowers are said to bloom in May and June. My impression is, however, that they go on blooming through the whole summer season, as do stocks. But I intend to consult a knowledgeable gardener, when I can find one. Of course," he added as an afterthought, "Emily may have indulged in a careless inaccuracy. What we sometimes sentimentally call *poets' licence*. But that is not my idea of Emily Brontë. Is it yours?"

"Mr Oldroyd," broke out Mellor, "I cannot bear to sit discussing harebells while all these awful things are going on in the world. Harebells don't matter."

"The attitude of mind about accuracy matters."

"Pettifogging," cried Mellor.

"Nothing is more falsifying, and only lack of goodwill is more damaging, in public relations than inaccuracy, whether about matters large or small. Using terms too large, too intense, too vehement for the matter in hand is a very dangerous form of falsification. One should endeavour to write and to speak with rational moderation to express the *exact* truth."

"We shouldn't get anywhere by being moderate."

"Where do you want to get, Mr Mellor?"

"We want a revolution!"

"A revolution by force?"

"If necessary."

"For myself, I regard revolution as a last resort, to be engaged upon only when all other methods have failed."

"That's pusillanimous," said Mellor hotly. "Why hesitate to try the only method which is effective?"

"But at such a human cost. When I think of revolution I always think of Zhivago walking along the side of a ripe cornfield. The field rustles, and he perceives that it is infested by thousands of rats."

"A cornfield——"

"Human food."

"Mr Oldroyd, excuse me, I don't wish to be rude, but you seem to me to be what my father calls a peace-at-any-pricer."

"I hope not," said Jonathan colouring. "Though I believed peace at any price was one of your tenets."

"Are you satisfied with the state of the world at present?"

"Certainly not."

"What do you think we should do about it, then?"

"The first thing that is required is thought. Careful, conscientious, informed—and of course, full of goodwill. Because of the immense population of the earth, and old animosities which still survive, our problems are difficult and confusing. We should *think* about them. Are you familiar with Hardy's *The Dynasts*, Mr Mellor?"

"No. We haven't got to Hardy yct," said Mellor youthfully.

"There is a very famous passage of poetry in the *Overworld* there, a Chorus of the Pities in which they plead for a more excellent way of life. It begins like this: *We would establish those of kindlier build, In fair Compassions skilled, Men of deep art in life-development, Watchers and warders of thy varied lands.* You notice these *watchers and warders* are *skilled* and have *deep art*."

"You only think in quotations," threw out Mellor hotly, and he banged out of the room.

The next time Mellor attended to have an essay returned —the course had now "reached", in his phrase, George Eliot, and the ethics of *Middlemarch* had given the young man ample scope for an attack on provincial society—he enquired of Jonathan what he thought of the ten commandments.

"That's a very large question, Mr Mellor," said Jonathan, laughing.

"No, but seriously, Mr Oldroyd, do you think they're adequate moral guides for the twentieth century?"

"They've worked pretty well for nearly two thousand years."

"But have they? Why should we be tied down by these awful prohibitions? Generation after generation, we go on having no fun. Why can't we do as we *like*?"

"Because other people also want to do as they like, and there must be some rule to limit our mutual intrusions on each other's rights."

"Primitive peoples get on all right without rules."

"On the contrary they're limited in every direction by taboos and tribal traditions. Civilisation is surely the liberating of the human spirit."

"I don't feel very liberated. Anyway, I don't think the Mosaic commandments fit modern times. The first, for instance, telling us to love God with all our hearts. If we don't believe there is a God, where's the point?"

"You love good, however?"

"Then there's all that about honouring your parents," continued Mellor, evading this question. "Nobody wants to do that nowadays, and Freud tells us why. As for the tenth, it's fine capitalist propaganda."

"I think it is the seventh which really vexes you," said Jonathan drily.

"Why not? Why can't we enjoy sex while we're young?"

"Mr Mellor, it might be useful to you to compile a list of ten commandments which in your belief, are adapted to twentieth-century conditions—but pray do it in the vacation, not in term," said Jonathan, laughing again. "Meanwhile, please note that George Eliot was quite as alive as you are to the stultifying inhibitions of provincial life."

A week or so later, at the close of a tutorial, Mellor hung back as the others left the room. With him were the stammerer and the girl in black network stockings. They all looked very serious, and Jonathan felt affectionately towards them.

"Mr Oldroyd," began Mellor, "could we have a word with you?"

"Certainly."

"What is your opinion of the value of student demonstrations in influencing public opinion?"

"A serious, silent demonstration would, I believe, have a considerable effect," said Jonathan. "But noisy catcalls and rioting, hustling, paper darts and the like, such as we saw in the Hall last night, have an adverse effect. They look too much like a student rag, youthful and irresponsible. Also when you see them reproduced on the television screen, as of course nowadays we all do, it can be seen that the students are laughing, either from mob hysteria or, what is almost worse, because they are enjoying the disorder they create."

"B-b-but do you agree with the sp-p-p-eaker last night?" said the stammerer.

F

"I disagree with him with all my heart," said Jonathan, speaking with passion.

The three pairs of eyes fixed anxiously upon him took on an expression of relief.

"Then surely we are entitled to express our disapproval of him," said the girl.

"Certainly. But in this country, free speech is the rule. He must be allowed to express his views, provided they are not incitements to hatred or disorder."

"I don't see why we should keep the rule if we don't want to," said the girl. "We can judge for ourselves what to do."

"The only true way to judge an action," said Jonathan earnestly, "is to turn it the other way round."

"How do you mean?"

"The speaker last night expressed right-wing views——"

"P-p-p-practically f-f-fascist," said the stammerer.

"——and you as left-wing believers, howled him down, and would have pushed him about if police hadn't prevented it. Now suppose the speaker had been left-wing, and right-wing students had howled him down and pushed him about. What would you have thought of that? Brutal interference? Illiberal oppression? Well? Tell me!"

"I think that's a cissy idea," said the girl with decision.

"It works though," argued Jonathan. "Murder and cruelty and lying always look wrong, whoever commits them."

"Then what are we to do to show disapproval?" said Mellor. "We can't just stand back and let these ideas grow."

"The best thing is to stay away from the meeting. But if you go, listen quietly, and at the end of the speech remain absolutely silent. Believe me, silence is far more crushing to a speaker, than any amount of noisy comment."

"I don't agree," said the girl quickly.

"Well, you haven't tried it."

There was a pause. "Was there any other point you wished to discuss?" said Jonathan mildly.

The trio looked at each other.

"We're going to London," said the girl at length. "On Sunday."

Jonathan, imagining that some question of Monday leave, over which he had no control, was involved, felt slightly puzzled, and was silent.

"To join in the students' protest march," said Mellor.

"We've hired a c-c-coach," said the stammerer eagerly.

"Will you come with us?" blurted Mellor.

"Of c-c-course we shall have to charge c-c-coach f-f-fare," said the stammerer.

"Will you come with us?" repeated Mellor harshly.

"If I do," said Jonathan after a pause, "my influence will be directed entirely against any kind of violence."

"That's what we want, isn't it, Peter? Isn't it, Dave?" said the girl.

The stammerer nodded. Mellor fixed his dark eyes, now burning with passion, on Jonathan's face.

"Will you come with us?" he said again, "or do you prefer to *speak not when the people listen*?" He paused and added with contempt "*Easy live and quiet die.*"

Under this taunt, the more bitter because it was a quotation such as Mellor had taunted him with using, Jonathan coloured.

9

DEMONSTRATION

IT WAS JUST before five o'clock on a cold October morning when Jonathan, having parked his car in the University car park, approached one of the large coaches which stood at the main Lorimer entrance. The coach lights looked cheerful in the autumn dark, and the hum of excited chatter round its door brightened his spirits. Some thirty, which grew to forty, young men and girls were clustered there, all of course hatless, most wearing long University scarves, and all clad in the anoraks and jeans which were the fashion of the time, or as near to these as their resources could afford. They all looked shabby, but as Jonathan had donned his oldest clothes himself he understood this; one did not attend a Demonstration, where one was exposed inevitably and shelterless to weather, sleeping in one's clothes, outdoor picnic snatches of food, and possibly shoving and pushing on a grand scale, in any garments whose preservation one valued.

Banners—bed sheets or stiff paper, wound at each end round poles which were probably broom handles—were now brought, unrolled and laid on the ground for inspection. They were inscribed with such prhases as U.S.A. OUT, LEAVE VIETNAM ALONE, THE SYSTEM IS ROTTEN, OUT OUT, and other such slogans. The printing, though large and legible, was so messy, uneven and altogether graceless, that Jonathan could not forbear a criticism.

"Haven't you any artists among you, to paint better banners? These are so hideous."

"If we had better banners, the authorities would say they were supplied to us," said Mellor angrily.

"By whom?"

"How should I know? We make these ourselves. We can't afford to buy them."

"That wasn't my point," began Jonathan, but his remark was lost in a sudden surge towards the coach door.

He had long since learned that leading must be done from the front, and that anyone who wished to exert influence must sit in front where his pupils could see him, and not at the back where he could see them. Not wishing to assert authority too obtrusively, he sank into the second seat from the front; Mellor and the stammerer were ahead, Mellor's girl, whose name it appeared was Alice Smith, seated herself beside Jonathan. He perceived that as the demonstrators entered, many of them gazed at him askance; he expected this and bore their glances cheerfully, but was not pleased when Mellor, after a moment's hestiation, rose and went down the coach and embarked on brief whispered conversations with some of the students, glancing from time to time in his direction. He deduced that Mellor's invitation to him was a tactic designed to respectabilise their participation in the eyes of the Lorimer authorities. After a brief resentment he decided that, very well, respectabilise it he would.

One or two latecomers came rushing breathless to the coach, which now appeared practically full, though in the confusion of people standing, changing seats, leaning over to talk and laying the rolled banners down on the aisle floor, it was not possible to discern the fact exactly. The driver, looking at his watch, expressed anxiety to Mellor, who rose and in his admirably resonant voice cried out:

"Sit down! Sit down! I want to count you!"

This was achieved; two seats were seen to remain empty. Mellor rose, and stretching his arms across the doorway to prevent himself from falling, leaned out and cried loudly:

"Any more for the Demo?"

Laughter greeted this from the coach.

"Shut up a minute!" shouted Mellor, turning to them. When silence fell, he leaned out again and repeated his cry.

No response coming, he withdrew into the coach and slid the door home.

"That's all, I guess," he said.

The driver nodded and started his engine. A loud cheer came from the students as the coach rolled off.

"Quite a good turn-up," said Alice to Jonathan.

"Yes, indeed. What time are we due in London?"

"Between twelve and one. We shall pause just outside London and eat our food in the coach."

"Ah," said Jonathan, ruefully conscious that he had not brought any food with him.

"We're due at Charing Cross at two."

"You have it all well organised."

"Of course," said Alice haughtily.

"Would you care to sit by the window, Miss Smith?" said Jonathan, making to rise.

Alice looked at him in astonishment, and said "No."

A loud outburst of eager chatter now arose, in which the word *revolution* figured so often that Jonathan began to feel soberly distressed. Mellor turning round and glimpsing the expression of his face, said sharply:

"Of course if you come with us you must expect to hear what we think."

"I shall be very glad to hear your views and learn your grievances," said Jonathan.

"It's gone far beyond student grievances," said Mellor eagerly. "Though of course we have plenty of those."

"What are they?"

"Lack of participation in the organisation of the University, and the curriculum. Well, the one springs from the other, really."

"I can understand and approve your desire for more participation, but I think professors who have devoted their whole lives to the study of a subject, know more about it than you do."

"But it's their view of a subject they teach. Students are taught bourgeois history, bourgeois economics," said Mellor, rising in his eager passion.

"And you want to be taught your kind of history and economics?"

"Of course."

Jonathan smiled rather sadly, and Mellor said with anger, "You're taught to conform."

"And you want to teach conformity to another system?"

"We want to be free to choose."

"Yes, freedom to choose and change!" broke in a student from across the aisle. "That we've never had."

"You are just reaching voting age, which will give you that freedom," said Jonathan.

By this time this conversation had become the object of general attention, and members of the coach began to join in from all sides.

"We want to give people control over their own lives!" shouted one from the rear.

"Yes. How passionately one longs for that in one's youth," agreed Jonathan, remembering his own longing *not* to go into textiles. "Great decisions one is entitled to make for oneself. In smaller matters, we always have to yield some of our desires to give room for those of other people, who also yield a little. It is the price we pay for living in communities. If we are to live amicably together we cannot have *all* our own way."

"But why should we give in to arbitrary authority?" cried Mellor.

"Some use of authority is necessary, if chaos is to be avoided," said Jonathan. "You yourself, Mr Mellor, used authority just now."

"I did not!" shouted Mellor, crimsoning.

"You told the students here to sit down and shut up—very wisely in my opinion," said Jonathan.

There was some laughter and ribald comment at this, and Mellor wishing, Jonathan thought, to restore his dominance, repeated very seriously:

"It's gone far beyond student grievances. Vietnam has provided a focus, a rallying point, a symbol. To smash the system at one point, we find we have to smash it at every point. The hierarchical structure is intolerable. We must continue our agitation until the entire present power-structure has been destroyed."

"What will you put in its place?" asked Jonathan. As Mellor exclaimed angrily, he went on: "No—I am speaking seriously. I really wish to know."

"Forms of revolutionary socialism," said Mellor, his eye glowing with enthusiasm.

"How will those differ from the present Welfare State?"

Mellor hesitated.

"We've been deprived of any revolutionary language in which to express what we feel," he said at length.

"I haven't noticed any lack of expression," murmured Jonathan.

He spoke quietly, because he saw that Mellor's ardent and idealistic, but turbulent and inchoate thought was indeed still struggling for form, and he felt a compunction about pressing his advantage.

Mellor turned and sat down abruptly.

The argument died. The stammerer, prompted perhaps by

Mellor, took advantage of the hush to go round the coach collecting fares. Daylight came, the coach lights were put out, the Midlands rolled by, flat, agricultural, interminable. Jonathan, observing that some of his young colleagues had already fallen to sleep, put back his head and attempted to do likewise. In fact he slept better than he had done for some time, for the pressing interest of his situation excluded the thoughts of his wife and children which usually so greatly troubled his repose.

They all awoke when the coach drew up in the park of one of those wayside cafés which the popular habit of touring has created. Rather cross at being thus jerked from sleep, the students stumbled out in a sullen silence, but after cups of tea and coffee revived. The occasion became jovial and noisy, and when they rejoined the coach songs were sung, by no means either unmelodious or inexpressive. Jonathan reflected that while the most respectable and middle-aged persons enjoyed the *Marseillaise,* the revolution which it celebrated being safely over, many of them would shudder at a song with a mournful cadence, each verse of which ended *In the fields of Vietnam.*

Alice Smith took the window seat without comment when they returned to the coach—whether for the view, the fulfil-ment of the fair-share belief, or the desire to appear independent of Mellor, Jonathan did not know; he was glad, but wished she had been gracious enough to mention the change he had proffered.

As they drew near London the students became excited and chattered vivaciously; then Mellor, imposing silence, described in detail the movements and meeting-places which had been arranged.

"It seems all very well organised," said Jonathan again to Alice.

"Of course," she snapped.

The coach drew up with a jolt.

"What's wrong?" cried Mellor.

"Police," said the driver laconically.

He rose and pushed back the sliding door.

A policeman—a Sergeant, Jonathan thought, or perhaps an Inspector; he was not well versed in police insignia— appeared at once in the doorway.

"All you young ladies and gentlemen going to the demon-startion?" he said cheerfully.

The coach roared an emphatic *Yes*.

"Then I must ask you to come out all together and allow my men here to search you," said the Inspector.

A horrified silence fell on the coach.

"Search us?" gasped Mellor. "What for? We're proceeding peacefully to a legal demonstration."

"Quite so, sir," said the Inspector.

"As citizens we're legally entitled to attend."

"Indeed, yes," said the Inspector. "But you are not entitled to carry offensive weapons. Our instructions are to see that you keep the law in this respect."

"This is intolerable," shouted Mellor.

"No, no, sir. Just a legal precaution. If you should happen to be arrested later, it would be much better for you not to be in possession of a weapon."

"He's right there," said someone from behind.

"We aren't carrying any weapons," wailed Mellor. His voice shook, his face contorted, he almost wept. "I give you my word." Jonathan felt with him.

"I might have a p-p-penknife," volunteered the stammerer.

This was received with hilarity by everyone except the Inspector, who stretched out his hand.

"Better turn it over voluntarily, sir," he said. "I'll give you a receipt, of course."

Subdued, the stammerer drew from an inner pocket a red-backed penknife. It was not tiny, but small enough to cause renewed laughter. The Inspector, enquiring name and address, wrote a receipt and handed it over.

"Any more knives?" said the inspector. "Any pins? Any marbles?" he continued.

His voice seemed to grow colder, and his eye more searching, with every sentence he uttered.

As the students were, in fact, completely innocent of any weapons, they all shook their heads emphatically. The Inspector appeared pleased.

"Then if you'll just step out, please. All together. As quick as you can. We don't want to delay you more than is necessary."

As Mellor seemed stunned, almost incapable of movement, Jonathan took his arm and without appearing to do so pulled him to his feet.

"We may as well lead the way," he announced cheerfully.

"I don't think I can bear this," murmured Mellor as they stumbled down the coach steps together.

"We're paying for the sins of those who *have* carried weapons," said Jonathan sternly.

But in fact he felt as keen a resentment, as furious a consciousness of unjust indignity, as Mellor. The policemen were perfectly polite, their handling was not rough, they kept their faces stiff in a wooden respect, but to have the contents of his pockets inspected, still more to have a policeman's hands running up and down his limbs, was almost more than the reserved and fastidious Jonathan could bear.

"This is odious," he said coldly to the Inspector.

"We're only obeying our instructions, sir," replied the Inspector with equal coldness.

Jonathan noticed that while the coach was empty other policemen searched it thoroughly, nor was even the driver exempt from this search. When at last the process was over and they returned to the coach, Jonathan felt at once alarmed and outraged, and he observed on the students' faces, as crimson with outraged anger as his own, the same mingled expression of fright and fury.

Indeed for the next few minutes they maintained a sullen silence; it was only when the coach turned sharply into a street which clearly led to an agreed parking place, for it was full of young students, recognisable by their college scarves, that they began to stir and chatter. Jonathan rose to his feet and turned towards the body of the coach.

"What a prig I shall sound, and yet it must be said," he thought, as he cried aloud in his voice of authority: "Just a moment, please."

Reluctantly, from habit, they fell silent and listened.

"In spite of this indignity to which we have been subjected, which naturally roused our anger, I know we are still all agreed that we must employ no violence. I must repeat this plain statement: if we use violence, we are exactly like those we are attacking for the use of violence. We are committing their sin."

He turned sharply away and busied himself with taking down his mackintosh from the rack above the seats. His heart was beating strongly from the effort of self-assertion, but he was pleased to find that without consciously intending to do so, he had said *we* and not *you*. He had thus identified himself with the students.

"Well, be it so," he admitted to himself, and all of a sudden felt cheerful.

The Lorimer students seemed to undergo the same cheering change of mood when, leaping from the bus, they found themselves in the midst of a milling excited crowd, laughing, shouting, waving arms and raising banners. Directed by students employing megaphones, they formed up and moved off in an orderly fashion, Mellor and the stammerer carrying the largest banner (U.S.A. OUT OUT) ahead, and the rest following, walking in rows with linked arms. Alice held one of Jonathan's arms and an unknown fair young man the other. As they approached Trafalgar Square the crowd increased, additions to its numbers pouring tumultuously in from side streets.

To his surprise, Jonathan heard French, German and some Eastern languages unknown to him spoken around him, and the faces he saw confirmed his view of the speakers' origins. Jonathan was a good internationalist and used to working with men of other nations; for a moment he found himself hoping that the more fiery emotions of other races would not overcome the natural Anglo-Saxon phlegm, but suppressed the thought as unworthy. Police were now lining each side of the street, and the students began to shout: "Ho! Ho!" It was a very shoutable and harmless slogan, and though Jonathan regretted that it had no specific meaning he found he enjoyed shouting it. As they entered the square a certain amount of surging to right and left took place. Alice was swept off balance, stumbled and fell to her knees. Jonathan and the young man on her other arm hauled her up swiftly and without ceremony, for to fall in a swaying crowd was dangerous.

"Are you all right?"

"Perfectly," she replied coolly.

Jonathan, however, observed that the black net stockings she favoured were both rent, and her knees were grazed and bleeding.

"There are some ambulances somewhere," said the fair young man on Jonathan's left.

"There's one over there," said the student on Alice's right, nodding to indicate the direction—he could not release his arm from the crowd's pressure to point a hand.

"I'm afraid we should have difficulty in making our way there," said Jonathan.

"Do you suppose I need medical attention for a graze on a knee?" said Alice scornfully.

"You should have an anti-tetanus injection as soon as possible."

"Oh, nonsense!"

The pressure now eased as students with megaphones again shouted instructions—"they have this all well arranged," thought Jonathan again—and a few short speeches now began. Jonathan listened with keen interest. It was not always easy to hear what was said, for though the crowd was silent, occasional buses and cars passed round the edges of the square and the inevitable shuffling of feet sometimes drowned the human voice, but he caught some of the same phrases he had heard Mellor use—*revolutionary socialism, arbitrary authority, hierarchical structure.* They were evidently current slogans. He felt that he was hearing, from some at least, not merely a protest against a specific war front but the expression of a genuine moral perturbation, a profound dissatisfaction with the current mode of life as materialistic, inhibiting and authoritarian.

"I agree, but what are we to put in its place?" he thought. "Is this just the same old argument caused by every techno-logical advance, which always hands more power to fewer persons? A Luddite question of machines, in this case electronic devices which produce an increasingly materialist society, against the participation of men? Is this revolt a step forward on the road to the liberation of the human spirit? Or a regression, a revolt against the disciplines which provide civilisation? A hatred of authority is natural. But submission to it, from herds of bisons and prides of lions up the biological scale to human groups, is natural too, to all animals who live in communities. We all want to do what we like. How to secure the maximum of this with the minimum disturbance of the rights of others? There must surely be some agreed laws—but they must be *agreed*."

A violent thrust sideways at this point almost threw him off his feet. Returning his attention to the outer world, he perceived that a considerable movement was taking place in the crowd, some sections, of which the Lorimer students formed one, swinging off vigorously to the right, whereas the main body curved down to the left. Reasonably but not intimately familiar with the centre of London, he decided that the Lorimer movement was certainly not towards Downing Street, where they were supposed to present a petition. He wondered why.

"Where are we going?" he enquired of Alice.

It was some moments before he could make her hear, for the crowd, though still not disorderly, were running and shouting and presently broke into singing. *The fields of Vietnam* rolled sonorously through the air, and the police who suddenly appeared to be lining these streets began to look rather grim. He shouted his query again.

"The American Embassy," shouted Alice in reply.

She laughed, her eyes gleamed with mischief.

"This is dangerous," thought Jonathan.

It was quite impossible to withdraw, however, even had he wished to do so, for the crowd surged forward at a half-running pace. He ran with it, pressed in on all sides, and devoted himself to keeping his feet and seeing that Alice kept hers. Alice was no doubt fully capable of doing so—she ran well and sturdily and seemed unafraid—except that from time to time she glanced back over her shoulder, and once even tried to turn round. This foolhardy manœuvre, annoying those who ran behind, was so unlike Alice's usual cool sense that Jonathan, as they turned a corner, tried to glimpse what had interested her. He saw the Lorimer group of banners, including Mellor's, scattered amongst the throng; having been in the lead, when the crowd turned they were naturally in the rear. Mellor could not move hand or arm to wave to Alice, nor change his place to come to her, but Jonathan perceived that he saw her and shouted some encouragement.

The students pouring into Grosvenor Square, and shouting as they caught their first sight of the Stars and Stripes floating above the grey building, now stopped suddenly. Jonathan, a tall young man, by standing on tiptoe saw the reason for this sudden halt. Rows of policemen—six or eight rows—firmly linked, arm to arm, faced the crowd, protecting the Embassy. Behind them were drawn up a row of mounted police, their horses and themselves sternly motionless. The serried ranks—*serried* is the operative word, thought Jonathan grimly—of police now took a slight step forward, their aim obviously to drive the students from the Square. The students perceiving this gave a great roar of frustration, and there was a strong surge forward. The police staggered back a step or two, but their line held. The students' charge was repeated, with varying strength and in varying parts of the Square, but with increasing determination. In the swaying back and forth, the jostling and shoving and pushing, Jonathan found himself in the front line of the argument, that is on the line of demarcation between students and police; he was thrust against the blue uniform and silver buttons. Now a shout of laughter broke out from the crowd; some daring students had climbed a neighbouring building, and one, half-clasped by a rather clumsy constable, snatched himself free and leaped from one balcony to the next. Jonathan, instinctively sympathising with the pursued rather than the pursuer, laughed as heartily as any. All the same he wished the students would retreat: they had made their point, had shown their disapproval, and they could not hope, or even wish, to penetrate six lines of police, and orderly dispersal would win more public sympathy than a scrimmage, meaningless and hopeless from the start. With some difficulty he managed to twist himself round with his back to the police, and searched the crowd for Mellor, who might initiate a move away towards Hyde Park, the arranged rendezvous. Long white sticks now came flying through the air towards the police. In some alarm Jonathan recognised them as the poles which had supported the student banners. Slight in themselves, when they descended from a height gravity would make their impact heavy.

"Don't throw those! It's dangerous!" shouted Jonathan.

At that moment a pole struck him on the side of the head. The blow knocked him sideways; he staggered and strove to regain his balance but could not. "No! No!" he cried, struggling—to fall was too absurd. He clutched at the person next to him but fell all the same; it was Alice; to his disgust he found his head jammed against her ankle, his blood seeping through her black network stockings.

Scrambling to his knees, he found her gazing down at him in horror.

"I do apologise," he said with strong sincerity.

"Now then, what's this?" said a police voice.

He was hauled to his feet and roughly dusted down. Struggling to extract a handkerchief, he accepted the one Alice proffered and applied it to the side of his face, which seemed to be bleeding considerably.

"If this were fiction, I should have a convenient blackout," thought Jonathan.

As it was real, however, he had to undergo in complete consciousness all the indignities of his situation. The police wished to take him off with them, the students were eager to use one of the ambulances they had thoughtfully provided. Mellor coming forward and asserting his acquaintance with the casualty, won the argument; students seized Jonathan's arms and pushed him through the crowd. Some of the students fell back from him awestruck and gasping, for the blood was very noticeable, others cried out about truncheons and police brutality; the need for continual repetition that it was an accident exhausted him. At last he found himself alone in an ambulance, which seemed to wander fitfully about the deserted Sunday streets of London. Alice's handkerchief was soaked; he discarded it and applied his own. After a few moments' relief at being quit of the jostling of the crowd, he began to feel enclosed and lonely, and had to exercise stern control so as not to give way to the fear that he had been forgotten and the journey would never end. It was an immense relief when at last the van drew up and the rear doors were opened.

"What hospital is this?" he enquired eagerly as he was assisted to descend.

"It's not a hospital, it's the London School of Economics," said the student who had driven him. "But you'll get medical attention here all right. It's all arranged."

Indeed quite a bevy of white-coated young men advanced upon him as he entered the building. Whether they were fully qualified physicians or last-year medical students was not certain, but they were certainly eager to employ their skill. The young man who attended to Jonathan was very capable —it was an immense relief to be mopped up, to feel clean and neatly bandaged; he insisted all the same that Jonathan should be driven off at once to the nearest hospital. There was some demur as to the need for this—clearly there had not occurred the number of casualties expected, almost, one might think, hoped for, and they were loath to let one go.

"Which would you prefer?" they said to Jonathan. "You can be properly cared for here."

"A hospital, I think," said Jonathan, who was beginning to feel extremely shaky and in need of some relaxing drugs.

No ambulance was available now, they had probably all gone off to Hyde Park and Grosvenor Square, but a taxi was found for him. After a further short but acute anguish of loneliness—he paid the driver with a trembling hand—a crowded bustling reception hall, a wander from desk to desk in search of registration, a wait of some minutes on an uncomfortable bench, during which he tried to listen with sympathy to an account of the ailments of an old man beside him, he achieved an interview with a doctor, who approved his bandage while removing it. It occurred to Jonathan to plead for a short rest before being returned to the outer world.

"I must catch the return coach to the north tonight," he began, "but——"

"Nonsense," said the doctor sharply.

Jonathan was peremptorily put to bed in a men's ward.

10

CONFRONTATION

FOR THE NEXT day or two he was so entirely occupied with his own bodily sensations, which were disagreeable, that he could not take time out for thought. He was wheeled about to be subjected to X-rays, and later taken to what he assumed was an operating theatre, for he was anaesthetised and emerged sick and miserable, with a numbed feeling in his head. Nobody told him what was wrong with him or what was to be done with him, but as he ascertained by trial that his arms, legs and ribs were intact, he did not trouble himself too much but allowed himself to sink into the luxury of rest. He had asked the L.S.E. students to dispatch a telegram to his professor—*greatly regret unable attend University for few days owing minor accident*—and left adequate funds for this; as he had visited his mother and the twins on the Saturday before the Demo, they would not expect to see or hear from him again till the following weekend. The left side of his face and head, including his left eye, was covered by bandages; fortunately he had no desire, or at any rate no energy, to read. On Tuesday afternoon, he was again carefully and skilfully transferred to a trolley, and this time wheeled off to an agreeable private room; he enquired what this meant from his nurses, one black, one white; they smiled kindly but could not tell him.

On Wednesday morning, however, things began to happen. He awoke to pain, but restored more nearly to his normal power of thought, and at once began to reproach himself for the idiotic anti-climax of his Demo adventure. To end up wounded by an accident, and hospitalised some two hundred and fifty miles from his home and work, was really too silly. He reproached himself and, as so often before, began to question his own motives in undertaking the action. He had not settled these to his own satisfaction, and had only just completed, with the dark nurse's aid, his morning ablutions, when a visitor was announced. This proved to be the Vice-Chancellor of Lorimer University.

"I came up for a meeting yesterday. I thought I would drop in and see you. I must hurry off for my train," said he.

Jonathan gazed at him in astonishment. The massive academic head, the spare erect figure, the look of accustomed authority, the urbane speech, indeed the well-cut, well brushed town suit, made a striking contrast with the starched print and cheerful brevities of the nurses.

"How did you know I was here, sir?"

"Oh, good staff work on the part of my admirable secretary. Tell me quickly how this accident happened."

"A flying pole from a banner hit my head."

"Poles don't fly without human propulsion. I presume somebody threw it."

"It was thrown up into the air, I believe."

"By a student?"

"Yes."

"A genuine accident?"

"Yes."

Jonathan wondered uneasily whether Mellor or some other demonstrating student had revealed Jonathan's whereabouts, and by doing so revealed his own participation.

"I still don't quite understand how you located me," he began.

"Your picture was in all the northern newspapers," said the Vice-Chancellor. "With the pole just clashing with your head. Very striking illustration." His tone was grim and Jonathan coloured.

"I'm sorry," he began again.

"You may well be."

"If you intend to follow the Guildford example," said Jonathan firmly, referring to the case of the Guildford Art College, where forty teachers had been dismissed for their assistance in a student sit-in: "I should be grateful to know it at once."

"My dear young man," said the Vice-Chancellor in a tone between irritation and amusement: "I haven't the slightest desire to terminate your contract. Your work at Lorimer has been good—I might almost say, very good. But the Senate won't care for assistant lecturers who take part in student demonstrations and tangle with the police."

"I didn't tangle with the police."

"Do you give me your word on that?"

"Certainly. The Lorimer students had no intention of committing any violence of any kind. We arranged that in the coach," said Jonathan eagerly.

The Vice-Chancellor seemed to receive this with some reserve.

"Your picture in the papers wasn't a good argument for that thesis," he said drily.

"I can assure you, however, that it was the fact."

"How long are you going to be in here?"

"About a week, I should think."

"Nothing seriously wrong?"

"I don't think so."

"Well, come and see me when you get back."

"Do you think you will be able to reassure the Senate, sir?" enquired Jonathan in some anxiety.

"Possibly," said the Vice-Chancellor, departing.

He gave a sudden grin as he spoke, however, and it occurred to Jonathan that it would be a bold Senate which went against this Vice-Chancellor's wishes. He smiled, disapproving of the hint of "influence", but reassured.

His next visitor was ushered in with a smile so approving that it had the effect of a red carpet. The man's strong stocky figure in solid dark coat and suit, new trilby and fur-lined gloves appeared at a distance unfamiliar; it was only when he drew near the bed that Jonathan exclaimed with pleasure:

"G.B.!"

"Jonathan! I am sorry to see you here. I would have come yesterday, but business in the House," began the man whom Mellor had stigmatised as one of those old fossils. They shook hands.

"Of course, you're a member of Parliament now; congratulations. Let me see, which is your seat?"

G.B. mentioned the name of his constituency, a northern industrial town with a large Labour majority. He looked so happy as he named it, so well satisfied, that Jonathan smiled with pleasure.

"You look very prosperous, G.B. Very different from the Luddite Mellor of 1812," he said.

G.B. frowned. "You would prefer us to look starving and ragged so that you could feel compassion for us, Jonathan," he said stiffly. "But we don't want your pity. We have strength and power and deserve your respect."

"In a word, you are the masters now."

"Why not? We haven't forgotten our ideals all the same."

"How would you define them exactly?"

"The protection of the right of ordinary people to have opportunity, security and education for the standard they are fitted to take. I don't want capitalism to have control."

"A quotation, I believe," said Jonathan, recognising the tone.

"Certainly. From Brother Cousins. I don't hesitate to quote from a better man than myself."

"He's not a favourite of mine," said Jonathan frankly. "I agree with his definition, of course, but tell me about the House of Commons. How do you like being there? Do you regret having given up your electronics? I suppose if Labour loses the next election you'll return to your profession?"

"Labour won't lose the next election," said G.B. smugly. "You won't see a Tory government in power in your lifetime, Jonathan."

"Well, that remains to be seen."

"Don't say you've changed sides and gone over to them, like Chuff!" exclaimed Mellor in disgust.

His horror was so great that Jonathan laughed.

"I remain what I've always been, a floating voter," he said.

"It's a pitiful position," said Mellor strongly.

"Still, I'm the sort of chap who swings elections and changes governments when they need to be changed," said Jonathan.

"You should stand up and be counted for what you believe in."

"That's exactly what I do."

"Well, I didn't come here to talk politics," said G.B. in a tone of kindly condescension. "Your picture was in all the papers, so I come to see how you are. What were you doing in Grosvenor Square?"

"I was marching with the demonstrators."

"That was very foolish, Jonathan," said G.B. as before.

"I seem to remember you approved of my marching with the C.N.D. against the bomb."

"That was different."

"Why? But never mind," said Jonathan hastily, not wanting another political declaration. "Tell me—your father's uncle, David Mellor—did he leave any descendants?"

"He was killed on the Marne, very young. He wasn't married."

"Ah," said Jonathan, nodding, and he decided to leave the Mellor relationships alone. Let them find each other if they could.

The nod gave him an uncomfortable twinge of pain, and he involuntarily allowed his head to sink back on his pillows.

"Is there anything I can do for you? I'm right down sorry to see you in this pickle, Jonathan," said Mellor, reverting to the idiom of their native county.

"No. I'm all right. Thank you for coming to see me."

They fell to talking of their young days in Annotsfield, and especially of Henry Morcar.

"I disapproved of him in every way, but he was a fine man for all that," said G.B.

"I agree. He knew his own mind and acted on it."

"He did that."

"He was an artist in textiles."

"I suppose so."

"My mother and I received immense kindness at his hands."

"There were reasons for that, as I understand," said G.B. diffidently.

"Yes. But my mother was not his daughter, as some people believed."

"Ah," said G.B. discreetly, nodding.

The Jamaican nurse put her head round the door.

"There are some other visitors to see you, Mr Oldroyd," she said, beaming.

"I'd best be off, then," said G.B.

He rose, shook hands with Jonathan and stated his London address and telephone number. The slight delay in his departure which this caused, brought Chuff into the room before he left it.

"G.B.," exclaimed Chuff.

"Chuff."

Both men spoke coldly and gave each other a hostile stare.

"Well, I'll be off," said G.B. He put on his hat and left with an abrupt and determined air.

"So here you are. Your picture was in all the papers," said Chuff, advancing to his cousin's bedside.

"I know," said Jonathan with a sigh.

"I would have come yesterday—I would have come on Monday," said Chuff with emphasis: "I telephoned, you know, but Susie would insist on coming too, and of course I had to fetch her and——"

"Susie!" exclaimed Jonathan. He sat up energetically. He felt as if he were suddenly alive again, warmly human after being encased for months in ice. "Susie! Is she—here?"

"I'll say she is," said Chuff grimly. "And not only Susie. I've got the whole caboodle with me. Susie would come, and then somehow the twins got to know—I'm afraid it was probably through young Hal, who is not particularly noted for discretion. So I had to bring *them*. Well, of course, I couldn't manage Susie and the twins alone, so I had to bring Ruth to look after them. Then you should have heard the howl my pair set up—you could have heard it all the way down the Ire Valley to Annotsfield. So Ruth insisted on bringing *them*, though they would have been quite all right left at home."

"I'm afraid it has been a costly affair for you," said Jonathan politely.

"Oh, pooh."

"What about mother?"

"She's in bed with 'flu, and Uncle Nat hasn't told her of your misadventure."

"Perhaps it was you," said Jonathan, suddenly enlightened, "who had me moved into this agreeable private room?"

"Well, yes. I telephoned the hospital and asked them to shunt you."

"Then perhaps you'll kindly have me shunted back into the ward," exploded Jonathan, furious. "I don't ever wish to enjoy any privilege."

"Jonathan, you are an ass," said Chuff with emphasis.

"Then kindly allow me to be an ass in my own way."

"Oh, certainly. You've done that already, anyway."

"Susie!" cried Jonathan, unable to control his impatience any longer.

Chuff's face softened.

"Well, forgive me, old chap," he said: "But we're using a device or two to keep Susie away for a few minutes. I felt I had to see you first, to see how you look, you know. We don't want Susie to have another shock, do we? Like when she saw father," he added in a murmur.

"And how do I look?" enquired Jonathan.

"Oh, not bad, not bad at all," said Chuff heartily. "That bandage covers you up nicely."

"Then let me see Susie," said Jonathan in a loud tone and with great precision.

"I'll fetch her."

At this moment, however, the door burst open and the four children charged into the room. The two boys coming in first, being commanded rather fiercely by Chuff to stand aside and make no noise, surprisingly obeyed, and stood by the washstand gazing in some awe at their bandaged uncle. The twins in bright blue tights and fur-collared suède coats to match, obviously winter wear provided by Ruth, rushed to the bed and threw themselves upon it, Linda as usual laughing merrily, Amanda with a quiet but ecstatic smile. They tucked themselves into Jonathan's arms and Linda began an excited and incoherent but vivid account of their journey to London, into which dogs, boys, porters and men

in white coats intruded. Amanda mildly corrected her from
time to time; it was a *black* dog, there were *two* men in
white coats, it was *Uncle Chuff* who said—and so on. Looking
from one to the other, Jonathan could not decide which
was the more beautiful. He hugged them both. Ruth now
came in, looking more matronly, more dignified, more
tastefully dressed and altogether handsome, though a trifle
less cheerful, than Jonathan remembered her. She offered
her hand.

"Thank you for everything, Ruth," said Jonathan,
clasping it.

He spoke in haste, for the Jamaican nurse, having looked
in and withdrawn at once in alarm, had fetched higher
authority to cope with the clamour, and it was now the ward
sister, in all her awful authority, as Jonathan reflected with
amusement, who entered the room.

"This won't do. This noise is bad for the patient. You will
all leave the room at once—except," conceded Sister as
Susie appeared in the doorway, "Mrs Oldroyd."

Ruth took her sons' hands and led them away. Chuff
picked Linda off the bed into his arms and carried her out.
Amanda quietly followed. Susie came forward and entered
her husband's line of vision. Jonathan with a deep emotional
exclamation sat erect and held out his arms and Susie hurled
herself into them. They embraced with passion, kissing and
embracing with all their strength. Susie, dressed (as usual
with exquisite simplicity) in a suit of an off-white colour,
seemed even more beautiful than her husband remembered
her. She wept tears of joy, and in her starry eyes Jonathan
read not the blank and frightened stare to which he had
become accustomed, but the loving gaze of a woman in full
command of her senses. They murmured endearments.

"My darling, how I have missed you!"

They said each other's names as if they were music, and

the surrounding scene, which had appeared so bleak and dull lately to Jonathan, was suddenly aswirl with rich colour.

"I shall look after you now, Jonathan," said Susie fondly.

"Yes, yes!"

They were still in the first ecstasy of reunion when Chuff came back into the room and stood looking at them with an expression of slightly sardonic pleasure.

"I'll take the twins home till you're a bit more settled," he said: "But I'll get one of the Hamsun people from our London office to put Susie up for a few days, then she can come and visit you reguarly, Jonathan. O.K.?"

"I'd rather stay in a hotel near this hospital," said Susie.

"I don't like to leave you alone," hesitated Chuff.

"I'm afraid I haven't much money with me," began Jonathan.

"Oh, pooh," said Chuff.

"This must end," said Sister, appearing again with a cross look. "I can't have my patient upset like this."

"It hasn't done me any harm, Sister, I assure you," said Jonathan.

"I'm afraid I must ask you to leave, Mrs Oldroyd," said Sister severely.

Susie with a sigh gave Jonathan a farewell kiss and rose— her movements were so graceful that Jonathan read a softening of appreciation even in the nurse's frown. Chuff hung back as Susie left the room, and it seemed to Jonathan that he exchanged a meaning look with Sister. He fidgeted with his tie, then approached the bed, drew a chair close, and sat for a few moments in sober silence, his hands hanging between his knees.

"Seeing you like this seems almost to have done Susie good," he said presently.

"Yes. Perhaps it has *broken her dream* as we say. She expected to see my mutilated body, like her father's, and found me instead alive and cheerful. It has destroyed, or at any rate mitigated, her fear of the accidents of life."

"Yes," agreed Chuff.

"And I think she feels now that I need her and that she can cope with that need."

"Yes, I'm sure that is so," said Chuff with more conviction.

"I will find someone to take the care of the children off her hands."

"Yes." He fell into silence again.

"Well, come, what is it?" said Jonathan at length.

"Well, Jonathan, I must tell you—perhaps better me than the doctor—I don't know—anyway, here it is," said Chuff. He spoke as if intensely embarrassed, and to Jonathan's astonishment drops of sweat broke out on his forehead. "Jonathan. You've lost an eye."

"What!"

"Of course the other eye is perfectly good. It will adapt itself after a time to single vision. You'll be able to read and all that—only perhaps with more care, less hours of use, I mean. No driving, I'm afraid. Susie"—Chuff gulped— "knows."

The shock was so appalling that for a moment Jonathan, stunned, was unable to speak. Then he suddenly felt that he must talk—about something else. He could not possibly mention his sight. But he must talk of something. He must conceal his anguish, he must direct attention away from this frightful catastrophe. The words babbled from his lips.

"You saw G.B. here, didn't you. So all three Luddite descendants were here. Your name's Morcar, Chuff, mine is Oldroyd, but I always think of you as more of an Oldroyd than I am."

"My mother was an Oldroyd, after all," said Chuff stolidly, accepting this conversational gambit with relief, but carefully not meeting his cousin's glance. "I always think of you as more of a Bamforth, Jonathan. Full of idealistic notions like the original Joe Bamforth. After all, you're descended from Joe's sister."

"We haven't made much progress in the hundred and fifty odd years since 1812," said Jonathan.

"Oh, surely!" began Chuff, "Everything's changed——"

"In our feelings, I mean."

"It's true G.B. and I don't care for each other much—we're enemies in a way, I grant you—but he hasn't tried to murder me yet."

"And I've not been hanged, but only lost an eye accidentally," said Jonathan, with a bitterness he could not suppress.

"Ah, Jonathan," said Chuff sadly. In an effort to return their talk to a safe subject, he added: "I suppose human vices stay pretty much the same down the centuries."

"And if so, human virtues are pretty much the same too," said Jonathan, brightening. "I mean, the old virtues are still valid, they only need to be differently expressed."

"You're an incorrigible optimist, Jonathan."

"Courage and honesty and goodwill," said Jonathan, becoming more and more cheerful: "They only need an adaptation of form."

"And what about chastity, eh?" said Chuff sardonically.

"We need a fresh conception."

"In more senses than one."

"Don't pretend to be a cynic, Chuff."

"No pretence, I'm afraid."

"This young man says he's come all the way from the North to see you," said Sister, entering abruptly. "Two minutes only, mind."

"Mr Mellor!" exclaimed Jonathan in surprise.

"I got a lift," said the young man, shamefaced.

Chuff surveyed him with keen displeasure. Indeed his appearance could only be described as scruffy. He was unshaven—which was forgivable; but his dirty face and hands were less excusable. His hair was unbrushed and untidy, his sprawling sideburns looked artificial, like theatrical wool; his short jacket of alleged suède was a good deal stained; his jeans were crumpled. But all this was nothing compared with the goodwill, and the effort, revealed by his presence.

"One of my Lorimer students, Chuff, who took part in the Demonstration," said Jonathan. "Mr Mellor, this is my cousin, C. H. F. Morcar."

"How do you do," said Chuff stiffly. Mellor sniffed and looked defiant.

"We heard you'd been carted off to hospital, Mr Oldroyd, but at first we didn't know which. Are you hurt, then?"

"My cousin has lost an eye," said Chuff, coldly furious. Mellor blenched.

"It was an accident," said Jonathan hastily. "One of the banner poles struck my head in its fall."

"Who threw the pole into the air?" demanded Chuff.

"Nobody knows," said Mellor.

He spoke in such hurried confusion that both Chuff and Jonathan became at once convinced that he had thrown it up himself.

"It was an accident," repeated Jonathan soothingly.

"What do you achieve by these silly demonstrations?" said Chuff. He spoke with contempt, because he found relief for his distress over Jonathan's disaster, in accusation.

"Nothing yet," said Mellor grimly.

"The struggle continues," said Jonathan with a sigh.

"What struggle?" demanded his hearers sharply.

"Self against Unself," said Jonathan.